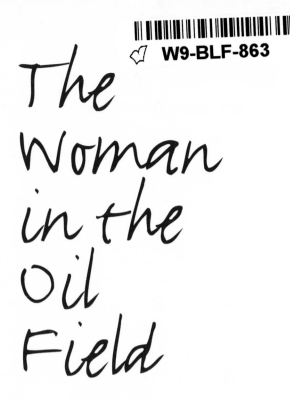

The
Woman
in the
Oil
Field

OTHER FICTION

BY TRACY DAUGHERTY:

WHAT FALLS AWAY

DESIRE PROVOKED

STORIES
BY
TRACY
DAUGHERTY

SOUTHERN
METHODIST
UNIVERSITY
PRESS
DALLAS

The Woman in the Oil Field

These stories are works of fiction. Names, characters, places, and incidents are either the product of the author's imagination or are used fictitiously.

Requests for permission to reproduce material from this work should be sent to:
Rights and Permissions
Southern Methodist University Press
Post Office Box 750415
Dallas, TX 75275-0415

Some of the stories in this collection first appeared in the following publications: "Low Rider" in the *New Yorker;* "Assailable Character" in *Ontario Review;* "The Woman in the Oil Field" in *CutBank;* "Four A.M." in *Gulf Coast;* "Almost Barcelona" in *New Texas '93* and the *Gettysburg Review;* "While the Light Lasts" in *New Virginia Review;* "Akhmatova's Notebook: 1940" in *Southwest Review;* and "The Observatory" in *Folio.*

Grateful acknowledgment is made for permission to use the following: Excerpt from "The Rum Tum Tugger" in *Old Possum's Book of Practical Cats,* copyright 1939 by T. S. Eliot and renewed 1967 by Esme Valerie Eliot, reprinted by permission of Harcourt Brace & Company; and quotations from *Anna Akhmatova: A Poetic Pilgrimage* by Amanda Haight, copyright 1976, reprinted by permission of Oxford University Press.

Library of Congress
Cataloging-in-Publication Data
Daugherty, Tracy.
The woman in the oil field : stories / by Tracy Daugherty. – 1st ed.
p. cm.
ISBN 0-87074-402-X (cloth).
ISBN 0-87074-403-8 (pbk.)
I. Title.
PS3554.A85W65   1996
813'.54 – dc20   96-26734

Cover art by Kristina Kennedy Daniels
Design by Richard Hendel
Printed in the United States of America
on acid-free paper

10 9 8 7 6 5 4 3 2 1

Contents

One

LOW RIDER

y name is George Palmer and my interest is insults. When I mentioned this to my wife on the day we met (she admitted later she disliked me at first) she said, "How come your parents didn't have any children?"

"I'm sorry?"

"That's an insult," said Jean. "Don't you get it?"

Lady, you have a fine personality, I thought, but not for a human being.

Actually, my field is insult *strategies* – social codes by which one group of people distinguishes itself at the expense of another. In Chaucer's day, for example, peasants told long humorous tales ridiculing landowners and lords. One of the most popular stories concerns a peasant commanded by an ogre to put his sheep to pasture. The peasant feigns stupidity and, by cutting off the sheep's tails and planting them in a field (as though the animals were head down in the dirt), pretends to bury the ogre's herd in the ground. The ogre believes his sheep have been slaughtered; the peasant sells the herd at market. With similar tricks he destroys the ogre's property, rapes the ogre's wife, and mutilates the monster himself. I told Jean, "I've got a good bedtime story in case we decide to have kids."

I'm rich. Oil money. Something Jean doesn't joke about. In 1941 my father and an Irish pal of his founded Ferguson-Palmer Oil in Midland-Odessa. Thirty thousand acres, wells producing three hundred to twelve thousand barrels a day. In '52 my father left exploration, bought the company's refineries, and moved to Houston where I was born. Our home was dominated by a ceiling-to-floor aquarium. A dark hallway led from the copper-paneled kitchen into a vast room, gently curved, the walls of which were made of three-inch glass. Muted blue light, languorous plants, soft living petals of purple and green. In recreating the Permian Period, when West Texas's major oil deposits formed, my father installed plastic brachiopods inside the tank and surrounded them with bass, catfish, rainbow trout. The room was his showpiece, his refuge from lawyers and accountants. When my parents were in bed I'd tiptoe down the hall, settle on a blanket in the flashing blue light, and let stripes of silver, orange and pink lull me to sleep.

As I watched the refinery workers from my father's office, my early awareness of insults grew. In front of the window he'd placed a bare table, a fence between him and the poisonous spires below. As a kid I crawled beneath the table, pressed my nose to the glass, and saw the men in hard hats stuck like spiders among the Xs, Rs, and Os of the pipes. One would raise his fist, another grab his crotch. Bare asses were proffered. Shouting, shooting the finger. One afternoon I noticed a young Chicano slapping the left side of his face with the palm of his right hand. The gesture, meaningless to me, was having an extraordinary effect on another worker, who danced precariously on a catwalk thirty feet aboveground and threw his lunch sack into the air with rage. Years later I learned that the *cara dura*, indicating cheekiness or undue provocation, was a common put-down among Latins.

In thirty-two years of production, Palmer Refining logged over a hundred and seventy-five thousand Man–Safe Hours. "Our hydrocrackers are as tight as battleships," my father told me. Each section of the plant, roughly three hundred square meters of intersecting pipe, was color-coded according to steps in the refining process (red meant distilling, yellow purifying, etc.). State law required seven fireplugs painted the appropriate color in each section. Sulfur and carbon, concentrated invisibly in the air, chipped holes in the parking lot, the workers' skin, and the paint, which had to be reapplied to the plugs every sixteen days: my first summer job. In my hard hat and jeans, turning orange, red, then blue, I inhaled Lucite and steam until my nose ached. At the end of the day the workers bought me Lone Star longnecks and cold ham sandwiches. In the smoke and dusky light of the bar they reveled in being offensive. Their leathery arms snapped up in gestures of anger and fun, but my body was so sore from the day's work I couldn't enjoy the jokes. The waitress traded amiable insults with the man behind the bar ("Hey Numbnuts, I need a sloe screw." "Have to wait, Babe, till the end of my shift") but I didn't catch them all. I'd become aware of *hearing* – just as at the plant, sniffing its awful fumes, I was always conscious of breathing – and my head buzzed with pain. I swore I'd never work for my father again.

As a graduate student at Indiana University, the center of folklore studies in America, I edited a small quarterly called *Heartland Folktales* and dreamed of starting a press of my own someday. My mother, an education coordinator at the Houston Police Academy, supported my decision. "Do what you want," she told me one morning. "You're rich. What are you worried about?" I'd been out of school for a month, and had come to ask her advice. She was relaxing on the police firing range between classes, pumping .38-caliber shells into the heart of a cardboard man. "You give a gun to a nineteen-year-old cop, send him to a one-room apartment in the middle of the night to stop a fistfight between a man and a woman, both drunk, who don't speak his language – *that's* worry. You, you're worth two, maybe three million dollars. What's the problem?"

Jean, a plasma physicist, forty-nine years old (and fifteen years my senior) always agreed: "I don't understand the point of your work, George, but if it makes you happy go ahead." Roy, her seventeen-year-old by a previous marriage, stayed in the basement spelling Able, Baker, Charlie into his ham radio, eating chili and drinking beer. I was free to edit manuscripts and to write essays on folk art for my Texas Republic Press, established in 1982 when my father gave me ten thousand dollars.

In the hair-curling humidity of Houston's hot afternoons I gladly went about my fieldwork. With a Sony portable cassette recorder whirring in my shirt I interviewed a retired postal worker who'd spent the last twenty-five years of his life erecting a monument to the orange. I talked to a woman who made plaster trees, lodging in their branches painted angels, Adam and Eve. I hung around with people on the margins of society, families visited by poverty and neglect: where folk art begins. I spent a lot of time watching kids. I think children have always lived in America's margins. As Germaine Greer says, "Drinking and flirting, the principal expressions of adult festivity, are both inhibited by the presence of children." Kids' folk art, I began to see, includes astonishing insult strategies, as in their rhyming games ("Liar, Liar, Pants on Fire," etc.). Each morning I watched a redheaded boy named Steven, the youngest of the children in our neighborhood, scream as the older girls teased him:

> Doctor Doctor can you tell
> What will make poor Steven well
> He is sick and going to die
> That will make poor Lisa cry
>
> Lisa Lisa don't you cry
> He'll get better by and by
> When he's well he'll dress in blue
> That's the sign he'll marry you.

Lisa was Steven's next-door neighbor, and nothing humiliated him more than having his name linked with hers, especially in singsong. The kids also established links through metaphor and simile: "Steven eats like a pig."

And direct statement: "Your father's a filthy plumber."

"Well, *your* dad's a midget Kung Fu spy!"

After lunch they often played leapfrog, with Steven as "It." He bent down and the girls jumped over him. The oldest girl, a skinny brunette of about thirteen who seemed to be in charge, was the first to jump; as she did so she tweaked Steven's ear. On the second pass she pulled his hair. Next time around she gave him a little kick, and so on. If any of the other girls failed to follow the leader she had to be "It." I recognized the game as "Gentle Jack," first noted in Edmund Routledge's *Every Boy's Book*, published in London in 1868.

"Possible topic," I scribbled in my notebook. "Steven, dismantlement of. His ego, his standing in the group . . . Playmates taking out on him what they often experience at hands of adults?" The game, I noticed, had a strong verbal component, to justify the physical abuse: "You're a turd, Steven. Your mother's a mouse."

"Components of insult run deep, poss. in all lives & encounters," my notes went on. "Purpose of folk art to remind us? Purp. of children?"

––––––

"I'm too old to raise another child," Jean insisted.

"It's still possible, though, isn't it?" I asked her one evening.

"You mean technically? Are all my cylinders still firing? Sure. But I've done the mother bit. This fall I'm on the tenure committee, the curriculum committee, the executive committee. Our peer review process for getting grants is breaking down in favor of congressional lobbying, and *that's* a fight we don't want to lose. I don't have time, George, not even for Roy. And you're out every night, God knows where, at your blues clubs or whatever. I don't think we'd be ideal parents."

She charged me with fostering an adolescent view of the world. "That's the trouble with poor little rich boys – sit around and dream, dream, dream. Sex, romance, the perfect little family. Daily life, George. It's stronger than anything. Dirty dishes, filling the car with gas, insurance bills, shopping for dinner."

She kissed my ear. "Stronger, even, than all those eager pictures in your lovely young head."

In the fall of '85, when she found out I was having an affair, she tore me out of every photograph we had of us together. "This is the *vilest* of your insults," she said.

"I've fallen in love. I didn't mean to."

"Well, then."

"I'm sorry. I'd like to stay."

"With me?"

"Yes."

"Stop seeing her."

"I'll try."

But Kelly and I continued to meet. She'd walked into the press office one afternoon with a newsletter, *Update: Central America.* "The Refugees: Who Are They?" the headline read.

"Can you print a thousand copies of this?"

"We're not set up for that kind of work," I told her. She rubbed her long white neck.

This Woman: Who Is She? I thought.

"Sit down. Can I get you some coffee?"

She represented the Central American Task Force, she explained, a group of citizens ("mainly women – men don't seem as interested") concerned about the violence raging then in Guatemala, Nicaragua, and El Salvador, and U.S. intervention in those countries – these were the high Reagan years. The Task Force shipped school supplies to San Salvador and seeds to Managua. They planned to leaflet every Wednesday in front of City Hall.

"Try Alphaset over on Richmond," I said. "They do bulk printing. They can probably get it out for you right away."

The following Wednesday at lunchtime I joined her on the street. Eight young to middle-aged women marched behind her in a circle, carrying placards: U.S. OUT OF NICARAGUA, HANDS OFF EL SALVADOR, NO PASARAN. Kelly, wearing a jeans skirt and a green blouse embossed with yellow parrot figures, handed newsletters to businessmen and women on their way to City Hall. "Get the hell out of here and stop disturbing the peace," a man told her. Kelly smiled. Conviction, controlled anger – a peppery combination, and it made me feel hot in my shirt.

She handed me a newsletter.

"Give me a stack. I'll help you pass them out."

Didn't miss a beat. "All right. You can work the crowd over there by the reflecting pool."

Four mounted policemen had cordoned off half a block for the small demonstration. "Whenever the Right Wingers march – the Klan or the anti-abortionists – the cops face the crowd so no one'll harm the marchers," Kelly told me later. "When *we* take to the streets they watch *us*, looking for excuses to break us up." Two men with long zoom lenses stood by a row of parking meters, aiming their cameras at us.

I offered a leaflet to a briefcase man. "Care for an update on Central America?"

"Fuck you," he said.

This happened three or four times. It was my fault; I couldn't keep the smile on my face. I understood their annoyance: who likes solicitors? Once, I was standing in line at the Astrodome waiting to buy tickets to an Astros-Padres game. A militant farmer shoved a pamphlet into my hand. "If you eat you're involved in agriculture," he explained.

"If you throw up," I said, "you're no longer involved."

He snatched back the pamphlet he'd handed me.

"Commie bitches!" a man yelled now from the steps of City Hall.

Kelly kept her friends in line – they wanted to tackle him, tear him apart, ship him in a CARE package under cover of night to a tiny island nation porous with recent democracy, yellow fever, and bent silver coins, massive market fluctuations and tsetse flies in the major export.

_____

"So what does a folklorist do besides ask nosy questions and stick tape recorders in people's faces?" Kelly asked once the newsletters were gone. We were sitting in a coffee shop across the street from the courthouse.

"What makes you think we stick tape recorders in people's faces?"

"I took a class as an undergraduate."

"Not true. We're very benign. Not a peep as we go about our business."

"Which is?"

"Watching."

"Is that why you showed up today?"

"No. I wanted to help."

"What do you watch?" She crossed her stunning legs.

"Anything anyone does. The way you're sitting right now. The way we're talking. Culture's always changing. Folklorists try to capture traditions before they disappear."

"Like from old people, you mean?"

"Sometimes." I put sugar in my coffee.

"It's a bit anal retentive, isn't it? Regressive?"

"No, you learn all sorts of amazing things."

"Like what?"

"There are two kinds of old people."

"Oh?" She smiled.

"Sure. There's the well-informed old person, good as any library. Then there's the talker. The talker may not be accurate, but the way he says what he says and the strength of his beliefs often tell more about the culture than any set of facts."

"When you get old you'll be a talker, right?"

"Why do you say that?"

"You came here to meet me, didn't you?"

"Yes."

"Do you have any interest in Central America? I mean *really?*"

"Of course." I ordered more cream. "They were taking pictures out there today – "

She waved her hand. "I've been photographed picketing the American Embassy in Managua. My file's a mile long."

In '85, when this conversation took place, Nicaragua was the Left's cause célèbre – flying into a war zone a sign of status, like owning a compact disc player or a VCR. It's astonishing to me how quickly the Sandinistas (and the American Left, for that matter) dropped out of U.S. news, swallowed by the fires of Eastern Europe and a leaky local economy, but back then everyone I knew had a strong opinion about them, one way or another. President Reagan even suggested they might attack America, starting with the little town of Harlingen at Texas's southern tip (there's nothing *in* Harlingen to occupy, except a couple of damned old Dairy Queens, maybe).

"This your first protest?" Kelly asked.

I nodded.

"Was it worth it?"

"You're interested in different cultures," I said. "I think you should come with me some night to hear the blues. I know the best clubs – black joints you can't get in if you're white. But they know me."

"Are you asking me for a date?"

"I guess I am."

"I should tell you," she said. "I have two children from a previous marriage."

"I love children."

"Is there anything you should tell me?"

I slipped a napkin over my left hand but she'd already seen the ring. "I don't know," I said. "Like what?"

———

"When are you going to work today?" Jean said.

"As soon as I get ready. Need anything at the store? I can stop off on my way home."

"Some Q-Tips. And a new ledger. We have to do the bills tonight."

"I wanted to stop by the lumberyard this evening."

"What lumberyard?"

"On 59. They're having a sale."

"What do you need lumber for?"

"I may want to build something."

She smoothed my thick blond hair and looked at me sadly.

"What is it?" I said.

"You're not going to build anything."

"Yes I am."

"You always say you want to build something. You never do."

"Well, now I am."

"You have to pick bill night to finally get started?"

"No. It's just that they're having this sale – "

"Every time I ask you to do something, George, you've got some idiot plan in the works."

"The problem is, you don't take me seriously."

She laughed. "No, because your job involves going out every night and getting drunk."

"I'm doing research at those clubs. The blues are a dying tradition."

"If I ask you just this once to stay home with me tonight and help me with the bills, will you do it?"

"The sale'll be over tomorrow."

"George, I need to go over the Amex receipts with you. You have to be here, okay?"

The ogre's endless demands: "Pick the vermin out of my hair."

When the idea first occurred to me to customize a car I was sitting in the Elm Street Blues Club listening to a local zydeco band and splitting pitchers of Old Milwaukee with two guys I'd just met. We wrapped our arms around each other. "I'm'one learn to play the pie-anny and join up with one of these-here bands," said the fellow on my left. He poked his red nose in my ear. "Make me a million bucks. Buy a brewery. And some beef."

"Hell, I'm going to *build* a piano," I said.

The other fellow was not a practiced scoundrel. I never did find out what brought him to the club that night in his three-piece Hart Schaffner & Marx, or why he felt compelled to join us in our joyful dissolution, but there he was, moon-eyed and slurry. He said, "I'm twenty-five years old, did you know that? It's a fact. And I'm going to tell you something. If I haven't made a million by the time I'm thirty I'm going to put a bullet through my head."

"There you go," said Red-Nose.

"And I'll tell you something else. I'm going to take as many people with me as I can." He made a pistol with his fingers and started picking off the couples on the dance floor. I poured him another glass.

"Get me a fancy car, or maybe an air-conditioned bus,

painted up so's it glows in the dark," Red-Nose said. "Play ever' toilet in the South."

"That's it," said the Suit. "A custom-made Eldorado and an Uzi." He twirled in his chair, made a screeching sound like tires and aimed his arms at the band. "Chuka-chuka-chuka," he said.

I went home drunk, woke Jean up and told her I'd had a vision of zinc-plated hubcaps.

"But those souped-up things are awful."

"It's folk art," I said.

Pots, pans, a dozen eggs. Cajun food always sobered me up before going to bed, especially if I concocted a major mess, got to flinging spices around the kitchen. I pulled a red snapper out of the freezer, defrosted it in the microwave, dipped it in flour and milk along with a medium-sized soft-shell crab. Oregano, basil, cayenne pepper. A little Tabasco.

Usually in these late-night gourmet sessions, to keep myself alert, I mentally ran through as many blues labels as I could: Arhoolie out of El Cerrito (later from Berkeley), Alligator in Chicago, Memphis's famous Sun. Howlin' Wolf; Son Seals; Clifton Chenier, King of the Louisiana Bayous. But tonight I kept picturing the car. I melted a pat of butter and saw in its golden bubbles shiny push-button door locks.

On Saturdays I sat in an unnamed café near the Ship Channel swilling Monte Alban from a bottle. Worms curled in the golden tequila, tugs moaned at the mouth of the bay. Dock-hands wiped their fingers on the cotton stuffing spilling out of the booth seats, and happily greeted one another: "Asshole!" "Pigdip!"

A couple of Hispanics from the refinery smoothed the way for me with old pros, young lions, and members of the gangs. With their help I built one of the classiest low-riders in the city: crushed-velours dash, red silk roses wrapped around the tape player, velvet Virgin of Guadalupe in the back window. In the trunk, beveled mirrors, strobe lights, color postcards of the Astrodome, a fully stocked wet bar. A selection of magazines for my friends: *Time, Outlaw Biker, Architectural Digest.* Hydraulic pumps in the rear, lowered suspension in front. Tru-Spokes, "French-In" antenna.

Following Mexican custom I paid a priest from Maria de los Angeles Church in southwest Houston to christen the "Anti-Chrysler" (the odometer was stuck on 666,666). He flicked Holy Water from a cup onto the red vinyl roof.

"Excuse me, Father." I wiped a stray drop off the hood. "I just Simonized that."

The car would bring me closer to ethnic understanding, I thought: a passkey to the barrios. Or maybe I was just showing off. In every part of Latin Houston I proudly displayed the Beast. In the northeast above Canal Street, Mexican families had opened groceries, *barbacoas,* funeral homes. The smell of smoked fajitas, lime-soaked onions, and fresh tomatoes drifted past grassy yellow tool sheds and mixed with the aroma of coffee roasting at the Maxwell House plant over on Harrisburg. Even the wealthy families here lived poorly, ashamed of ostentation. Their Caribbean cousins rented modest brick homes in south Houston, near Martin Luther King Boulevard. I drove the Beast through these neighborhoods early one evening and made a lot of friends. Parched lawns, naked kids chasing the Paletas del Oasis, the Popsicle man whose tin-fendered truck played "Georgia on My Mind." Most of the Dominicans worked for Macon and Davis, on the nuclear plant north of town. On Sunday afternoons the men (full round faces, high cheekbones, coffee-colored skin) sat among saints and ceramic animals in their living rooms cheering José Cruz. *"He's rounding second, rounding third . . ."* In the kitchen, sausage and plantains, barefooted women chopping pineapples, whispering about the *tigres,* the "bad men" who demanded protection money from families in the neighborhood.

Koreans were now running most of the old Cuban markets, I noticed. The Cubans, getting poorer, were probably migrating to another part of town, but that wouldn't be clear for another couple of years.

Eighty to ninety thousand Salvadoran refugees lived wherever they could, anonymously in the suburbs or at shelters in Montrose and the Heights, partially gentrified neighborhoods where Kelly taught English twice a week.

"How'd you get involved with Latin refugees?" I asked her one night.

"Well, you can hardly grow up in Texas and not be aware of Hispanics. I've always loved the people, even back when I was a little girl. They have the most appealing, handsome faces."

On Wednesdays she worked late at Casa Romero, the largest of the shelters. I'd fix dinner for her daughters: Monica, seven, Kate, five.

One night Monica pulled a deposit slip out of a drawer and drew an animal on it. "George, guess what this is."

"An ostrich."

"No."

"I can't guess, sweetie."

"Yes you can."

"Are those legs?"

"Uh-huh."

"A zebra."

"No!"

I put the cauliflower in the oven.

"Guess, George."

"*Monica*, I'm trying to make dinner."

"Guess!"

"Okay, give me a hint."

"It lives in the water and has fins and long legs."

"I don't know."

"It's like a beaver."

"I give up."

"It's a beaver!" She laughed.

"Beavers don't have fins."

"Yes they do."

———

"Did you tuck the girls in?"

"Yeah. Kate's full of energy this evening." I stroked Kelly's breast.

"Wears me out."

"Are you sleepy?"

"I'm afraid I am. Long day. We had a fire at the Casa."

"You're kidding."

"Found some rags in the basement. Kerosene."

"Who'd want to burn the place?"

"Lots of folks. People in the neighborhood. There's some old guys who've lived there twenty, thirty years. They're real unhappy about all the Latins moving in. And the cops are always dropping by, waiting for us to provoke them."

"Anybody hurt?"

"No, we caught it before it did much damage, but life's getting spooky. Like those fundamentalist freaks blowing up abortion clinics."

I kissed her forehead. On the wall above her bed, a world map; thumbtacks in every country from which she'd had a lover. "How many have there been?" I asked, pointing up there now.

"I'm not sure. I lost count somewhere down around Bolivia. How're things with Jean?"

"About the same."

"You could move in with me."

"I could."

She yawned. "I don't know why you married that old woman anyway."

———

Jean was working on a theory that the smallest particles in the brain – which she called "morphemes," in deference to my dumb grammarian's mind – are trapped fragments of the human psyche, just as matter is a form of trapped light. "Life is electrified activity in which every particle strives to return to pure energy – an unagitated state," she told me in bed one night. "The easiest way to do this is to attract one's opposite. This movement, of course, dooms each particle to solitude. If it finds its opposite, it dies. As long as it searches, it remains unfulfilled. For every feeling of love there's a feeling of fear. These are physical, palpable things, George, I'm convinced of it. Fear *is* matter. And matter's free when it returns into light."

"I kind of like the shape it's taken here." I squeezed her thigh.

She lighted a candle and turned off the lamp. "Do I bore you with my theories?"

"No."

"One of the worst things about being nearly fifty years old is that life holds few surprises for you." She cupped herself around my ass. "There's very little I feel excited about anymore. When I latch onto a new idea I tend to get carried away."

In the mornings she rose early and did fifty push-ups and fifty sit-ups. On Tuesdays at noon she had an aerobics class. In the evenings she liked to throw a softball around with me in the park. She'd developed a strong arm.

"I'll do everything," I said in the park one afternoon, returning to my old subject. "Feeding, nurturing – "

"Doesn't track with reality, bucko," she called back, whacking her mitt. "Babies just naturally go for the mother. We have the milk."

"It'd be different with an adopted child. They prefer a fuller menu."

She fired a fastball into my mitt.

"Ow."

"Even an adopted child would imprint on me. I'm just not willing to do it."

I watched Mustangs, Impalas, and Gremlins shuttle by on the freeway down the hill from the park. On an overpass someone had painted "War Pigs in Space." A few miles away, helicopters lowered white stretchers onto the gleaming glass towers of the medical center.

Jean picked up the bat. "You need to decide if you're committed to this marriage before we start talking seriously about adopting a child. Because if we *do* have one, then you run off with your little Leftie, that kid is your responsibility, not mine. I won't get stuck at my age with being a single mother again – Roy's enough." She tried to hit me a pop fly but the ball sailed over my head. "I told you you'd get tired of me. That day on the golf course, remember? I knew then why you were coming on so strong."

"I *liked* you."

"It was the novelty of seeing an old woman who could wear a pair of shorts."

"Jean – "

"Oh, I have a very clear-eyed view of myself. I have nice legs, but I'm forty-nine years old. You can't hang on to that beautiful young body of yours forever, you know? Golden belly, strong thighs – they're not yours to keep. You don't know what that means yet. Believe me, it's a shock."

"Let's go get some ice cream."

"Wake up one morning – "

"Okay? Jean?"

She started to cry.

"For God's sake, you're talking to me the way you talk to Roy," I said. "I'm just trying to make things smoother here."

"My breasts sag, George! I have these handles on my hips! I told you that." She threw the ball in the dirt. "Why didn't you listen to me? Why didn't you leave me alone?"

———

Kelly exhausted and drawn. Another fire at the Casa. They'd lost the whole kitchen and one of the downstairs bathrooms.

"I have to go back there," she said.

"It's after midnight."

"Can you stay with the girls?"

Monica and Kate were wide awake. I made some hot chocolate.

"Where's Mommy going?" Kate said.

"She has to take care of some business."

"George, remember that pony we saw at the stable? With the brown spots on his back?"

"No, honey, I wasn't there."

"Yes you were."

"Your mother took you to the stable by herself."

"No she didn't."

"Did so." Monica shoved her sister.

"Snotty snotty snotty."

"That's enough, you two."

Kate grabbed my hand. "Remember his bulgy eye, George? Was his eye sticky?"

"I don't know, Kate. Probably."

She tugged my fingers.

"Yes, honey, what is it?" I said.

"Mommy says you live with another lady."

"That's right."

"Why?"

"Because she's my friend."

"Better friends than us?"

"I've known her longer than you," I explained.

"My robot can turn into a truck. Want to see?"

"Okay."

"I don't like her," Kate said.

"You don't know her."

"When are you gonna live with us?"

"I don't know."

"I'll help you clean your room," Kate said.

"Thank you, sweetie. I appreciate that." I kissed her cheek.

"George?"

"Yes, Kate?"

"This lady?"

"Her name is Jean."

"She's like a grandmother, isn't she?"

"What has your mother been telling you?"

"She says she's about a hundred and fifty years old."

"Not yet."

Kate sat on her foot. "Does she really have wrinkles on her butt?"

———

Late one night three plainclothesmen arrested two Salvadoran women at Casa Romero and charged them with selling amphetamines.

"They were diet pills," Kelly told me afterward. "Laxatives. It's a war of nerves. They're trying to crack us bit by bit. They've subpoenaed our files."

"You've got nothing to hide."

"Harry, one of the volunteers here at the house . . ."

"What?" I said.

"He made a couple of border runs."

"Jesus. Illegals?"

She nodded.

"You told me – "

"I know, but these were desperate people."

"How many trips did he make?"

"Three."

"The INS'll have a field day."

"I'll need you to babysit from time to time, but I think we'd better cool it, George, until things blow over. I don't want you getting mixed up in all this."

"Kelly – "

"I mean it."

She was always firm when it came to her plans. I knew I couldn't change her mind. I'd miss spending afternoons at the Casa. The place looked like a take-out barbecue joint – had, in fact, been a restaurant. A Pepsi-Cola bottle cap painted on the side of the house was starting to peel, smoky in the shade of four white oaks. Red cedar picnic tables sat in the front yard next to a gravel drive. Newspapers and old fliers, wrapped in rubber bands, nestled in the high, wet grass. It was homey.

One day at the shelter I'd talked to a thin Latin woman with dark scars on her arms. "Who did this to you?" I said.

"The *Guardia Civil* in San Salvador."

"Why?"

"They took my husband. I was passing his picture around in church."

The beige hall carpet smelled of cat pee and vomit. Wallpaper hung in strips, an old-fashioned dial telephone sat on a cardboard box in the corner.

I pulled a notebook out of my pocket. The woman rocked back and forth on the floor. "Tell me," I said.

"The men in masks, they force you to worship their whips, their fists. They give them names," she said. " 'The Enforcer,' 'The Lollipop.' " She rubbed her arms. "After many beatings these words are the only ones left in your head. Your own name has been taken away from you. You've betrayed the names of your family and friends. Water hurts, light hurts, clothing hurts. But the hardest pain is not when they hit you. It's when they make you stand for many hours." She squeezed her legs. "Alone, in a room. You begin to hate your feet."

Water trickled through a pipe inside the wall. "The body –

its own enemy?" I scribbled. I recalled, as a kid, painting the fireplugs at my father's refinery: the soreness that stayed for weeks in my back and arms, the weight of sitting and walking.

Insults to the body.

The woman closed her eyes. The hatred and suspicions that characterize put-downs had begun to hit too close to home. I thanked her for speaking to me.

I followed Kelly's wishes and stayed away from the Casa. Most days I worked at the press or just drove around. One afternoon I went to the Shamrock Six, Houston's worst movie theater, and bought a ticket to a movie called *Hollywood Student Hookers.* I never knew, in advance, what was playing at the Shamrock, or what time the films started. I came to watch the audience: predominantly black, several generations bunched together in the seats – Great-grandad in the middle, Mom and Dad, festive kids spilling ice on the floor. Everyone talked to the screen.

"Don't go *in* there you fool, he waitin' for you!"

"Now you gonna get it."

"Yo ass be grass."

A circus of insults.

Hollywood Student Hookers had been playing for half an hour. I took a sticky seat. A woman shot a man in the face.

"I *tol'* you, sucker," someone yelled at the screen.

I sat through two showings of the film, greatly enjoying the crowd. Afterwards I swung by Prince's for shakes to take to the girls.

Twice a week I babysat Monica and Kate while Kelly tutored her English students. One day I took them to the "Orange Show" on Houston's east side. That retired postman I'd interviewed had built a monument there to his favorite fruit, using scraps, pieces of farm equipment, and masonry tile. Winding metal staircases, red umbrellas, Texas flags. Stages for music and puppets. I loved to see the girls in my car, the way they sank into the seats like little dolls. Before we'd got in the Beast for this trip, Monica had cut the side of her foot on a sliver of glass in the street. Kleenex and tears.

"George, I'm bleeding on my shoe."

"It's all right, honey. Press down with the Kleenex."

Kate shot passing cars with a straw. "Our daddy was supposed to call us last night but he didn't," she said. She liked to comb the Chrysler's goatskin seats.

"George, I can't walk!"

"When we get there we'll get you a piece of ice to put on it."

Ten minutes later she was running up and down the metal stairs. It was late afternoon, with a full moon low in the sky.

Watching the puppets, Kate leaned her small body against my back, resting her head on my shoulder, asking questions about the action onstage.

"What's that clown doing?"

"Reading."

"Reading what?"

"A letter from someone very far away."

"Farther than the end of the street?"

"Yes."

"Farther away than the moon?"

"Just about."

"Oh," she said, twisting around into my arms. "When will my daddy call?"

"I don't know, Kate." Kelly's ex was a traffic engineer in San Diego.

"I go see him in the summer."

"I know."

"We go swimming." She crawled off my lap. I showed her the evening star.

In the next three weeks, fourteen Salvadorans, eight Mexicans, and a Guatemalan boy were arrested at the Casa, on charges ranging from burglary and smuggling to possession of illegal substances. Casa Romero was ordered closed, its furniture impounded. Deportation proceedings began against nine of the Latins.

"I'm going to Arizona," Kelly told me one day soon after.

"What's in Arizona?"

"Harry has some friends there who're setting up a shelter. Desert community. Sympathetic to the cause."

I touched her knee. "Are there freeways in Arizona? I'm not happy unless I'm on a freeway."

"I know." She smiled sadly.

"You're sure?"

"Yes. I want to do this."

"I'll miss you," I told her, stunned.

"Me too." She tried not to cry. "You're a real good talker, George."

Driving through the barrios, gazing at graffiti on old city walls: U.S. OUT OF GUATEMALA, U.S. OUT OF WESTERN EUROPE, U.S. OUT OF NORTH AMERICA.

A kid on a bike shot me the finger, out of the blue. I laughed. How could I leave this place, this seething gumbo of spicy, bad behavior? Houston was more than just the city in which I lived. It was a spot whose intricate culture, whose social codes I'd cracked.

I called Kelly from a pay phone and told her I'd live on Fritos if she left. "I'll waste away . . ."

"You're being deliberately cruel," she said. "Come with me."

"What would *I* do in Arizona?"

"Open another press. Write books. I don't know, George."

"You think I don't have a life here, is that it?"

"It's certainly not a life you can't improve on, is it? Is it?" she said. "Look at the hours you keep. The crap you eat. Here's a chance to start over, to lead an intelligent – "

"Intelligence has nothing to do with it," I said.

When I thought about my children, I imagined them in ten-pound, double-ply fertilizer sacks at the back of the garage. If I talked Jean into having them – a boy and a girl – I'd cut the baling wire and let them out.

"You're late," she said. I'd been driving around all day. My eyes were swollen from crying. "Supper's in the fridge. Where've you been?"

"Running errands."

She'd been working on her computer. "George?"

"Yes?"

"How worried should I be?"

"What about?" I put my hands on her shoulders from behind. She touched my fingers. "I don't know," I said.

She turned the desk lamp away from her face. "When I got married the first time, my husband and I seemed perfectly matched," she said. "Emotionally, intellectually, temperamentally. Our goals were the same. We each wanted a nice house, dinner parties on the patio. But right after Roy was born I felt this desire to go back to school. I couldn't understand it. I'd never been ambitious for a career. What had changed?"

She placed her elbows on the desk. "Now I think people get married for very specific reasons. Roger wanted someone to arrange his social life. I wanted a child. Beyond those things we had nothing to build on. I guess I'm not sure marriage is functional after a certain point. It has a half-life of maybe five years."

"What did you need from me?" I asked.

"I wanted to feel sexy again."

I kissed the back of her neck.

"Do you know what quarks are?" she said.

"Subatomic particles, right?"

"Do you know where the word comes from? *Finnegan's Wake.* Guy who named them thought it was a nice-sounding nonsense word Joyce made up. Turns out, in German 'Quark' means something like 'cottage cheese.'" She turned off the lamp. "I can't seem to make sense of – "

"Shhh."

Crying softly against my shoulder.

———

Kelly was leaving on Saturday night. "It's crazy to cross Texas in the heat," she said.

I touched her chin. "You have the smoothest skin . . ."

"We'll leave around nine, from the house. I hope you're there."

I squeezed her hands.

"You won't be, will you?"

I didn't say anything. She kissed my cheek.

Saturday afternoon I drove for hours in the Beast, into the piney woods then south along the NASA road. I felt as groundless as an astronaut reeling in a dizzying orbit.

Around six I stopped at a place I knew called Grady's and ordered a chicken-fried steak. On the bar TV the Mets were thrashing the Astros. I ordered a pitcher of beer. When the baseball game was over I played a little pool, threw some darts. Bought another pitcher.

Ten-twenty. My stomach tightened. *You asshole*, I thought. Maybe she'd waited. I could leave all my clothes . . . buy a pair of shorts down the road.

I was kidding myself. My mind had been set all along.

Mike, the bartender, said, "Rack 'em up, George. I'll give you a lesson in eight ball."

I rubbed my eyes. Stood. Swayed. Jean would wonder where I was if I didn't phone soon. "All right," I said. Mike put a quarter in the table and the balls fell out: a thunderous boom.

"You break," Mike said.

"Sure."

We squared off across the room. Too much beer. The table swirled. Solids, stripes, slats in the floor, golden bottles, canned laughter from the television speaker. Mike shuffled his feet, waiting for me to start. "George?" he said. I chalked my cue, gazed at the tip. Bright blue dust rose into the air, shimmied, filtered down onto the smooth green table-carpet . . .

I remembered telling the girls stories at night to get them to sleep. I remembered sitting with them on the porch at Casa Romero talking to a young Salvadoran woman. Above us, cicadas caromed off the eaves. "They get in," the woman said, proud of her English, "when you open the door." I remembered trick-or-treating – Monica dressed as Madonna, singing "Like a Virgin," Kate wearing an Albert Einstein mask. She gripped my hand. "It was the scariest one in the store," she said.

Assailable Character

Six months before my daughter Jessie was born I found a Japanese Bobtail crouched under the still-warm engine of a red Ford Galaxy. I'm partial to just-parked cars – the soft ticking of their motors as they cool, the waves of heat, the freshly pressured rubber hoses. On any given night I can spot the warmest, snuggest automobile in my neighborhood and nearly always find a cat there, purring, trying to force its way up inside the transmission. The night I found Meckie I was roaming the streets of Bowling Green, Ohio, looking for cats with more than five toes on each foot. My wife Susan was finishing her political science degree at a local university; I was teaching a high school biology class and researching a mutant gene called polydactyl, which can produce as many as eight toes per paw. For some reason, 15 percent of the cats in Boston, Massachusetts have extra toes. While Susan huffed and groaned with the weight of her pregnancy I furiously wrote grant proposals for funding to Boston and to Nova Scotia, where evidence suggests the odd gene may have originated.

The wind gets spooky in Bowling Green in late October. It carries a chill from Lake Erie and a scent of oil and steam, but brackish somehow, as if from sunken ships. I was always hungry in those days: since the middle of her second month Susan had refused to shop or cook. She'd developed a taste for pickled okra, a particular brand from Texas. She sat in front of the television taking little bites out of the jar, tossing the hard stem ends into a shoebox she'd set by her chair for that purpose. I didn't mind quick trips to the store or kitchen duty, but I didn't keep a regular schedule. Most evenings I'd just heat some frozen eggrolls for dinner. "If you're going out, bring home a bottle of peanut oil," Susan called one night as I left the house with my pockets full of cat chow. "Or some Cheez Whiz. I'd like to try it on my okra."

I walked to a nearby corner grocery and saw the red Galaxy parked in front. I'd never been beneath a Galaxy. Spitfires were my favorite – a good seven inches between the engine block and the ground. Delta 88s weren't bad, either. I heard a plaintive whine and bent to look. A black and white kitten. She didn't want to leave the metal's warmth; she'd backed herself up to the right front tire and was sharpening her claws on the axle. I lay beneath the bumper with her, cozy, out of the wind. The owner of the car came out and chased us both down the road.

On the way home the kitten slapped my ankles, snagging one of my socks. I named her Meckie after Mack the Knife in *The Threepenny Opera*. Her claws were like blades. Susan cried because I'd forgotten the Cheez Whiz.

She accused me of not wanting the baby.

"What do you mean? Of course I want the baby," I said.

"You always leave the house after dark. Where do you go?"

"Just walking. The Dorfmans've bought a brand-new Mazda. It's a little cramped underneath, but the engine traps heat."

"You're unhappy living here with me."

"Sweetie – "

"It's horrible, admit it. My awful urpiness in the mornings – "

"I'm with you. You know that."

"Even my fingers are fat," she said.

I kissed her forehead. She touched my arms. Meckie had scratched the hell out of my wrists; the marks appeared as though I'd taken a razor blade to myself over the bathroom sink.

Ultrasound: the first snapshots of our daughter. Dr. Potts, Susan's obstetrician, a big man with skinny lips, spread the images on his office desk for us early one morning. All I could see in the pictures were two blurry bars, like a pair of unsharpened pencils, and what appeared to be a series of holes surrounded by rippling waves. The computer-enhanced compositions reminded me of bleak Scandinavian paintings I'd seen in art classes in college – impressionistic studies of people screaming on rocky, violent seashores.

I pointed to one of the pencils. "Is that a penis?" I asked Potts. "We're going to have a boy?"

"That's the head," he said. His ears were padded with tufts of hair as pale as his papery skin. "I can't be certain, but my guess is you're looking at a lovely little girl."

Susan beamed and squeezed my fingers.

In the Honda on the way home I carried the ultrasound prints in my shirt pocket, along with a grocery list: *Cheez Whiz, cat food, Ajax, scallions* . . .

Susan wouldn't let go of my hand. Today she was happy about the baby. Jessie hadn't been penciled in on our calendar, but when we first got the news we decided to forge ahead. We'd always talked about raising a child someday. We reasoned that, eventually, most good citizens marshalled their genes and produced worthy heirs – it was one of the things that *made* them good citizens.

Susan raised my hand to her lips and kissed my bitten nails. "We'll teach her to wipe herself gently so she doesn't get a rash," she said, "and to go easy on the coconut when she's baking a cake because coconut's expensive now at the market, and we'll show her how Peter Jennings's face is more trustworthy than Dan Rather's, though they'll both be wrinkly by the time she's watching the news, and we'll impress on her – "

The edges of the prints nudged my skin through the thin cotton fabric of my shirt. I shivered.

A bulky cop stopped us at a crosswalk a block from our house. Healthy-looking children with all their limbs in place ran across the street, clanking their *Back to the Future* lunchpails against perfectly formed little thighs.

Behind us a woman in a rumbling Pontiac lined her mouth with lipstick. She appraised herself rather critically, I thought, in her rearview mirror. I fantasized walking back to her car, opening the passenger door, and sliding in beside her.

"And we'll teach her to curtsy and to pray, and to have – " Susan caught her breath and gripped my hand till it hurt. " – unassailable character. Right, Josh?"

The decision to have a child comes from a deep and private place in the heart, the part that holds marriage sacred, that honors long-range planning and decent behavior. And despite these family pillars, you're never really sure if what you wanted was actually a *baby*.

I tried to be happy. I tried to prepare. And all the while I was thinking, "Holy God, we're going to be swimming in shit."

Susan taught me a prayer to pass on to the child:

"Angel of God – come on, Josh, do it with me."

"My guardian dear," I recited.

"To whom God's love."

"Entrusts me here."

"Ever this day . . . Joshua, *ever this day . . .*"

"I forget."

"Be . . ."

"At my side."

"To light, to guard."

"To rule and guide."

Lately she prayed I'd do something with Meckie before the baby moved in. "The Knife," as we called the cat (two of our quilts were in tatters), had grown into a good, solid hunter.

Each day after school I'd come home to find pulled-apart little creature-hearts on our porch.

"I won't have our daughter crawling through diseased former *things* on the floor," Susan told me one night.

I was chopping daikon for a Chinese dinner. Chinese had been Susie's favorite before she'd started craving okra. "Let me work with her," I said.

"You can't work with cats. They're untrainable. You, of all people, should know that." She looked at me.

"What is it?" I said.

"I was wondering what kind of daddy you'll make."

"Shall we trot out all my flaws? They're in a bag here somewhere – no no, those are the mushrooms . . ."

She laughed. "Our little girl'll be screaming for supper and you'll be out with your head up a Rabbit's ass."

I liked to hear her laugh. "Help me clobber these carrots, will you?" I handed her a knife. "I'm ready for her, Susie. I'm ready for anything."

"How do you know?"

"My dreams," I said.

Usually my past returned in sleep. Like videotapes, my dreams replayed hard facts and added very little by way of imagination or editorial comment. Often at night my mind recalled the trips I'd taken on research grants: Barcelona, where I once found a rare wire-haired Balinese under an I.R.A.-brand delivery truck, Iran in the Shah's last year of power. Behind an outdoor market in Tehran I'd followed a beautiful blotched tabby down a dead-end alley. The cat had whorls instead of stripes, an uncommon marking in the Middle East, and I wanted to note its gender, the state of its health, etc. Two SAVAK agents picked me up and took me in for questioning – strange behavior, they said. Suspicious character.

But last night my dreams had been different. "Forward-looking," I told Susan. "In one dream I followed a slender Siamese under a classic white Fairlane. When I poked my head beneath the bumper, the oil pan started to leak and out popped a baby drenched in 10-W-40. 'Papa,' she said. 'Take me home and show me the good life, with Mars bars and lots of TV.'"

Susan shook her head. "A good father wouldn't let that old thing in the house." She pointed at Meckie. "And a *really* good father'd promise not to leave – "

"Ah," I said. "I see."

Susan frequently complained about my field trips – my "animal habits," she called them. She also said I didn't make enough money. Absolutely true. "If you joined an honest-to-goodness research institute, instead of teaching, you'd have more security and benefits," she said. "You're thirty-four, Josh. We need to be more settled." Also true – and the only course of action now that we were about to have a child. But I liked chasing cats around the globe. It kept me on my toes, and made me feel younger than I was.

―――――

One evening, late in her second trimester, after a wheezy, throbbing day in which Susan had had second thoughts – about the baby, about me, about virtually the entire planet (oddly, these black moods were always followed by weeks of maternal rapture) – I snapped a picture of her in the bath. Dime-sized bubbles of soap wavered and popped on her belly. "It's all over for me," she said when she saw me with the camera. She mourned her lost youth. "From now on, it's chicken broth and buckets of drool." At that instant she looked to me more sensual than ever. Radiant and pink, with her red hair pulled back. I wanted to cuddle under a Buick with her. "Talk to me," I said.

"It's your fault I'm this way."

The flashcube sizzled.

―――――

Perilous, the first year of our marriage. Several near breakups. I hated to remember it now, but I couldn't forget in light of this permanent bond, this pencil-shaped new person that was about to be visited upon us.

Our joint therapist had once described Susan's restlessness as "low-level depression." He said she was suffering from poor self-esteem, stemming from her childhood (her father was a stern Lutheran minister). "Until she corrects her self-image," the doctor told us, "she can't be happy." This may have been the case, but it seemed to me at the time that Susie's biggest problem was low-level horniness: a constant mild ache, wherever she was, to run her hands along the naked flesh of a stranger.

I was fairly well-acquainted with this sort of thing myself. But I felt that a person had to be disciplined, otherwise you left sticky messes in your wake.

For months after we'd introduced ourselves at college we circled each other warily. She was dating someone. A banker. *My* banker, as it happened. I was seeing several women. We felt an attraction, a grab, at the very least a tug – the emotional equivalent of a stubbed toe, perhaps. We had a series of coincidental half-meetings in restaurants and malls, hurried conversations, and one night, when we both failed to float safe excuses, a half-attempt at sex. Susan stopped us. She was still partially committed to the banker, she said, and could only go so far.

I began to call her every day. I suggested we meet in disaster areas (earthquakes, tornadoes) where buildings and electrical power had been halved. We could sit together in candlelight, I said, sipping straight Half-and-Half (leaving it unfinished, of course) and listen to bootleg tapes I'd bought in high school. I had the Beatles in rehearsal: they ran through parts of songs, then quit. "I'll only wear half my clothes if you'll just wear half of yours," I said.

I had no romantic illusions about Susie. I was never intrigued by the mystery of unattainability. I simply felt lucky and at home when I heard her voice.

After the wedding she'd sometimes insist, "I never wanted a husband."

"Then why did you marry me?" I'd say.

She wouldn't answer. She'd just look at me and repeat, "I never wanted a husband."

I went to the vet and asked her if I could prepare Meckie for the baby, so that animal and child wouldn't be in each other's way. She gave me a short list of tips.

1) *Before the Big Day arrives, expose your cat to small infants. If you can't find a neighbor baby ask relatives and friends to videotape their children. Play the tapes for your pet.*

2) *Familiarize your cat with baby smells. Powder, food, clothes.*

If possible, bring home a dirty diaper and let the cat get acquainted with the scent.

One night I called Frank Peterson, the vice principal at the high school where I taught. His wife Janet had just had a baby. "Frank? Joshua Storey here. Fine, fine," I said into the phone. "Yeah, I heard, that's great. Susie's eight months along herself. I know, they get that way – "

"Get what way?" Susan snapped.

"Listen, we have this kitty over here, and I was wondering if we could borrow one of little Michael's diapers, a soiled one, yeah, to show it . . . oh sure, we'd wash it before we brought it back," I promised.

Susan dog-eared her copy of Henry Kissinger's *American Foreign Policy,* on which she had an upcoming exam. "For God's sake," she said. "Haven't these people heard of Pampers?"

3) Set up the crib before the infant arrives and train your pet to stay away from it. Otherwise, the cat may want to sleep with your child.

In a tiny room just off the kitchen I cleared a space next to the washer and dryer, built the crib, hung pink curtains, and taped up several pages torn from a Dumbo coloring book I'd found at the store. I sat in a corner of the room gripping a water pistol, a finely detailed German Luger, and squirted Meckie whenever she came near the crib. She glared at me, hatefully. "Screw you both," I said to my wife and my cat on particularly bad days. Susan wasn't talking much. Okra stems lay in the shoebox at her feet. I called my mother for advice. "Be patient with her, Josh. Her body's going through changes."

"You're telling me. She's as big as the World Trade Center."

"What are you feeding her?"

I glanced at the box. "Size nines," I said.

———

"What will our baby look like?" Susie asked me one night. "I mean, genetically speaking, what are the possibilities?"

"It's hard to predict," I said. I pictured various members of our families. "She could be big as a battleship or small as a bath toy."

Susie wasn't pleased. She was so large by now she couldn't haul herself out of a chair without my help.

One evening after dinner she wanted to take my picture. "With your shirt off," she demanded, posing me by a window.

"Why?" I asked.

"When our daughter's old enough to appreciate men, I want her to see how young and sexy her father was."

"Somehow you just made me feel old."

She popped a flashcube onto the camera. "Flex your muscles, Josh. A little Schwarzenegger action."

"Our kid's going to think her parents were pornographers," I said. I was depressed. That morning I'd resigned my post at the high school, effective at the end of the summer. Bio-Systems Research, Inc. of Toledo, Ohio, a small outfit on a farm road south of Lake Erie, had hired me to write grant proposals at three times the salary I was making as a teacher. Instantly I'd become a better potential father in Susie's eyes, a more upstanding citizen, but my schedule looked daunting to me and I wouldn't earn a vacation for another two years.

"Glad to have you on our team," Wayne Miller, my new boss, had told me at lunch. "We've been trying to bag federal dollars for months. We're going to need you 'round the clock here at first."

I was going to miss chasing cats. With my long hours I feared I'd miss seeing Jessie grow up.

Susie circled me with the camera, standing on tiptoe or crouching (sort of), as though she couldn't see me.

"Josh?"

"Yes?"

"Smile."

In Buenos Aires, shortly after the military coup in March '76, I saw a gorgeous gray Angora with only three legs, limping from car to car. Under the tense scrutiny of several heavily armed young soldiers, I coaxed the cat out of a jeep and took it to a vet. It was one of the happiest moments of my life.

In the days before Jessie was born I'd lie in bed with Susan, rubbing baby oil on her belly, trying to calm her fears about the world. "Our little girl'll be so helpless . . .," she'd say. I practiced my lullabies on her, from *Old Possum's Book of Practical Cats:*

> The Rum Tum Tugger is artful and knowing.
> The Rum Tum Tugger doesn't care for a cuddle;
> But he'll leap on your lap in the middle of your sewing,
> For there's nothing he enjoys like a horrible muddle.

The night Susan gave birth I decided I couldn't be a father after all. I'd driven her (fumbling with the gear shift, finding fifth when I wanted third) to the hospital early in the afternoon, but Potts said it was a false alarm. "She'll probably be in labor yet for several hours," he told me.

The maternity wing's waiting room was empty except for myself and two other expectant dads who'd obviously been through the process before. They seemed relaxed, and were having a mild argument about the causes of sudden infant death syndrome.

I found Potts again and asked him what I'd miss if I left for twenty minutes. "Go get yourself some dinner," he said. "She'll be all right."

At home I treated Meckie to half a pound of mozzarella. (I *had* been saving it for pizza, but Susan informed me that morning we'd have to start watching our calories – "For the baby's sake," she said. "We need to stay fit.") I stood in the middle of the kitchen with the grater in my hand, and let the cheese filings fall to the floor. Meckie purred around my ankles.

After my hot pot pie I took a walk around the block. The red lights of the radio tower at the end of our street darkened nearby roofs; the tower's guy wires creaked. A cold lake breeze gave me goosebumps. I didn't know my neighbors very well but I'd become intimate with their cars. Tonight the Moore's Datsun was warm. Its windows were down – the interior smelled of French fries. The Ryersons had finally washed their station wagon.

Yellow lights burned in windows up and down the neighborhood. Dinnertime. Squash, potatoes, beets. I felt keenly the rhythms of the families around me.

In Fred and Alice Dorfman's level drive I noticed a plastic baby doll, left by their daughter after play. The driveway was spotted with oil. I recalled the dream I'd had about the Fairlane, but this coincidence didn't startle me as much as the doll itself. Its features were lifelike and lovely. And *casual.* As though infancy, or birth itself, could be taken for granted – a notion so at odds with what I'd felt for months now, I became disoriented and somehow frightened.

I lingered in the street. Then, I remember, I ran back home, switched off all the lights. I hopped into the Honda and raced without thinking through town. Video stores lined the highway. Life-sized cardboard Rambos stood in the store windows, preening. Slick muscles and guns. Several filling stations appeared to be failing along this strip of road. Owners had taped hand-lettered signs to their pumps: "Sorry, No Gas."

In a gravel parking lot just outside the city, teenaged boys crumpled cans of beer. They carried bowling balls in rhinestone-studded bags.

I imagined my daughter sitting beside me in the car, her umbilical cord wrapped like a seat belt around her waist. Take a look around, Jess, this is it, I thought.

Diesel trucks kicked up dust in my lane. To my right, the tattered husks of old drive-in movie screens. The torn white canvases on which actors used to dance, kiss, sing, flapped now in the breeze like huge cicada shells.

Past fields of mint and wild onion I drove. Their loamy smells stung tears into my eyes. For a long time, with the radio on, I didn't slow down or stop.

———

Sometimes when you've been joking with a friend, then you shake hands and part, you may still have the trace of a smile on your lips – a little facial echo of a happy moment. That's how Susan looked in her hospital bed when I walked into her room from the nursery.

She reached out her hand to me. The space around her pillow smelled of roses (I'd bought a dozen at an all-night Safeway when I'd driven back to town) and rubbing alcohol.

"Hi," I said. I kissed her eyebrows.

"Have you seen her?"

"I've seen her."

"Does she have all her fingers and toes?"

"Yes, and she came with her own little American Express card."

Susan smiled. "Josh," she said.

"I love you," I said.

"I think I want to rest for a minute."

"Okay," I whispered. "Angel of God – "

She squeezed my hand. "My guardian dear . . ." But she slept before I reached the next line.

———

This afternoon the baby and I lie on the floor staring in delight and disgust at the Knife's latest gift: a half-dead pigeon, one wing meekly thumping the carpet. I say, "We'd better get this out of here before your mother sees it, Jess."

But Susie's standing in the doorway, laughing, with the camera. She's quit fighting the squalor that baby and pet and an occasionally still-ambivalent husband – not to mention her own uncertainties – have brought to her life. She's not very good with the Kodak; heads and feet tend to be missing from her shots. I once read that cats (depending on their gene-patterns) can't see many colors. They can't tell gray from green. Complex shapes are fairly easy for them to resolve, but they can't distinguish human faces.

Meckie stares at me as though I'll snatch her catch. She's right. Then I'll vacuum the carpet.

But first, I think, I'll lie still for a while. It's pleasant here on the floor. I watch my wife twist the lens and try to pull our daughter into focus.

MUSTANGS

esterday Philip, my nine-year-old, found my old drum set in the closet. The cymbals had turned pale green. They sounded like tin. The snare rattled and wheezed. "You play?" Philip asked.

"I used to. In junior high and high school."

"Why'd you quit?"

"Grew up. Got busy."

"You could've been on MTV."

"I wasn't that good," I said, though my riffs were snappy enough, in the spring of '69, to shake his mother's hips at a high school dance.

Philip weighed an old pair of sticks in his hands. He bashed the hi-hat with delight. "How much did this stuff cost?" he asked.

"Not much. I pieced it together over a couple

of years, mowing lawns." A Gretsch tom-tom, a Slingerland bass drum, a Yamaha snare. Ludwig cymbals. As a beginner I used a matched grip, holding the sticks like two hammers: that's how Ringo did it, and that was good enough for me. The music teacher at school told me this wasn't the "proper way to be percussive."

"The sticks must oppose each other," he said. "The right one straight, the left one held like a fork. Tension and opposition are what give the music fire. Like the act of passion, do you understand?"

I said I did, a little.

I'd joined the junior high marching band, the Pride of the Mustangs. We wore green and white uniforms and hats with plumes. We marched in parades through the city.

"Where was this?" Philip asked. "In Texas?"

"Yes." Midland, Texas. Twenty years and half-a-country away from me now.

I remember, in the ninth grade, in the big Thanksgiving Day parade, I dropped my left stick as the band turned a corner on Main Street. I couldn't stop to pick it up – the trombonists were right behind me with their dangerous slides. Elephants and horses and shitting zebras followed our fat little twirlers, marching steadily in broken rows. For several blocks, until the parade was over, I kicked the stick ahead of me.

The marching snare, strapped to my left leg, pounded my right knee whenever I high-stepped: black and blue for the sake of the beat. Mr. Webber, the band director, drilled us after school on a practice football field, yelling at us through a cardboard megaphone whenever someone made a mistake, rehearsing us for hours in sun or wind or rain. From him, I learned the most I'll ever know about self-discipline.

But in those days, when I was just a little older than Philip is now, I wasn't interested in discipline. I yearned for girls and a life of rock and roll – until the chilly night, one winter, I fell in love playing "Me and Bobby McGee" behind a sad young lady named Ida Mae Weaver.

It happened this way. I had a friend named Jackie Waldrip. He played French horn in the Pride of the Mustangs but his hero was Jimi Hendrix, and he'd bought an old Gibson guitar at a yard sale. When marching season was over, we practiced Beatles tunes in my garage after school. Jackie knew a couple of other guitarists, whose names I've forgotten now, and we formed a "pop quartet" – that's what the fan-zines called the boy-groups who were topping the charts of the day. Psychedelia was at its peak then – this was '67. We called ourselves "Crystal Creation." I drew an exploding diamond on a piece of poster board and taped it to the front of my bass drum.

Jackie was a quiet kid with a sorrowful demeanor, even when he smiled. His brown hair looked like pigeon feathers, plucked and scattered. Musically, he was much more gifted than the rest of the "Crystals," but he always deferred to the bass player on arrangements. I thought the bass player was a moron. He knew zip about song structure and didn't even *own* any Beatles albums. Jackie adjusted to my pace even when I rushed a phrase. He looked up to me, though with his skills and gravity of presence, he should've been the leader.

My mother brought us iced tea and Mars bars whenever we took a break. "You sound real good, boys," she'd say, trying to hide her smile.

We always rehearsed in my garage because it was large and new. My father was an oil man – which is what I've since become, running pipe up to Alaska out of Portland, Oregon – and we had a nicer home than most of my friends. Jackie never talked about his parents. I hadn't been to his house. I got the idea that his folks embarrassed him somehow, or maybe they were sick or something.

Often he'd stay for dinner after the other "Crystals" had left. Baked squash was his favorite food. That's one of my strongest memories about Jackie Waldrip – I don't know why. "He could eat a pound of this stuff," my mother told me. "Don't they feed him at home?"

After dinner we'd play records in my room and talk about the girls in our classes. "Peggy Sue Rittenour is named after the Buddy Holly song," I told him one night. This fact made her exotic to me. She was the first girl I ever tried to date – though my efforts embarrassed us both. At the spring prom the year before, I'd been too shy to ask her to dance. All night I smiled at her from across the dance floor/gym, but I wouldn't come close. She stood with her circle of friends. One by one they approached me and said, "You're breaking her heart," "I hope you're happy – you've made her miserable," or, "Cretin."

I felt as foolish as when I'd dropped my stick.

Just as I'd worked up my nerve to speak to her, the band announced its final tune. Peggy Sue started to leave. In a panic – I had to make a gesture – I rushed up to her, pulled a quarter from my pocket (all I had) and said grandly, "Here, take this!" It wasn't until months afterwards that I realized she might've been offended.

"Kissing's enough," Jackie said. "That's all I ever want to do. It gets ugly after that."

I wondered how he knew; I'd never seen him talk to a girl. "What do you mean?"

"You know. What *you* want to do, and what *she* wants to do, and would you like to go to a movie tonight, and which one, or would you rather study? It's complicated."

"Yeah," I said, fearing I'd never get close enough to even smell a girl's perfume. Dance floor etiquette was already more than I could handle.

———

Music wasn't the only activity I shared with Jackie. Twice a month that spring we interviewed a small crew of Mexican roughnecks on an oil rig east of Midland. Our English teacher had assigned his students to tape and transcribe conversations with folks from various social classes, then compare their speech patterns. I knew vaguely what "social classes" were, but people were people, I figured, they simply worked different jobs. Back then, I didn't know the angers and economics attached to those differences. Jackie did – and I think now the story I have to tell is partly one of class.

As I've said, I didn't know much about Jackie's background. I knew he wasn't poor, but he didn't share my world of privilege. My dad was no Rockefeller but he *did* work in the deal-making branch of oil; I was protected to the point of naivete from the harsh lives most people lived in the West Texas desert.

For middle-class speech I taped my own parents. My teacher's brother owned an independent drilling company. He let Jackie and me and some other kids talk to his workers to complete our assignment. We took a bus to the oil field after school. The Mexicans were all in their twenties, energetic, weathered by sun and gritty wind. Their muscles were fine and tight, like the sinews of the wild green mustang painted on our bass drum at school. Neither Jackie nor I felt completely at ease with the men, but he stood among them with a kind of calm, a rough grace that (I see now) signified a kinship of class. Without knowing it I revealed – in my thick cotton shirt, my Buster Brown shoes, my "proper" stance – the money my father made.

What we discussed I don't remember, except that most of the workers had left their families in Mexico and worried about them. I'd heard ranchero music on KCRS late one night – the cheery accordian solos and the polka beats – and wondered if that's what these men listened to. I tried to find some point of contact with them, but they didn't seem to know what I was saying. Jackie did most of the talking. His communication, I recall, consisted mostly of a strong, sympathetic silence.

————

One day, as we were walking home from school, Jackie asked me if I'd like to go to his house. "To practice, I mean. Could your mom bring your drums over in the car?"

"Sure. We can call the other guys from my place."

"No. Let's just do it ourselves today."

He lived in an old neighborhood out by the rodeo grounds. Slatless blue shutters framed the windows; the cracked cement porch was painted red. Behind the house, on a dusty track inside the rodeo arena, three young girls ran horses through an obstacle course built around seven yellow barrels.

Jackie's mother looked a little like a barrel herself. Her neck was huge. She wore fuzzy houseshoes and a purple cotton muumuu. Her shoulder-length hair was square-cut and blond. She hefted my bass drum with one arm, picked up the snare with the other, and carried them into the house. "It's a shame the other boys couldn't make it," she said. I looked at Jackie. He toyed with his amp. I understood that he was ashamed of this woman and trusted me to be quiet about her, in a way that he couldn't trust the others.

Mrs. Waldrip said she was a songwriter. It turned out, she'd asked Jackie to bring his "little rock band" over to practice a tune she'd composed. "Writing's really a cinch. They got these rhyming dictionaries, see?" She picked a paperback off an old piano in a corner of the den. "Let's just look up 'spoon,'" she said. "Rhymes with 'June,' 'swoon,' 'boon.' Ain't that a kick?"

She settled her bulk on the piano bench, sipped a sour-smelling drink from a Smucker's jar, and taught us her song – mercifully, I've forgotten it. We sat there all afternoon, improvising what she called the chorus.

"I'll tell you what I'll do," Mrs. Waldrip said when we were done. The room had grown dark. She'd had several drinks. "I know a man over in Odessa who owns a recording studio. For eight bucks an hour you can rent it. He'll produce a demo tape for us – hell, we sound good, just the three of us, don't we? Who needs a bass-line? We'll make us a demo and send it around to all the record companies, won't that be wonderful? Which label does Bobbie Gentry sing for? This song'd be perfect for her."

"I'd better call my mom now," I said.

Jackie wouldn't look at me.

The next day, on the oil field bus, he apologized. "She wants to practice again with you and me."

"What about the 'Crystals'?"

"When we do the demo, she'll get this record-business out of her system."

"We're not really going to record her song?" I said.

Jackie shrugged. From the bus windows we saw the horselike men hoist heavy pipes through bright steel rigging toward the sky. Jackie watched intently. Over and over the men squatted, lifted, heaved, and tugged until I felt certain their bodies would break.

———

I don't recall how many weeks passed before Mrs. Waldrip phoned my mother to ask if she could "borrow" me for the evening. I hadn't told Mom anything about her. I knew if my folks learned how much she drank, they wouldn't let me see Jackie again.

Around six o'clock one evening the Waldrips pulled into our driveway in a red Chevy wagon. I'd never seen Jackie's father: a small man – or rather, a tall stooped man, twisted by whatever tools he used at work. Tiny broken veins formed faint kaleidoscopes on his cheeks. He shook my hand. "David," he said. "I've heard a lot about you."

"Yessir."

We loaded my drums in the rear of the wagon. Mrs. Waldrip promised my mother they'd have me back by ten at the latest. My mother was excited. I think she thought her son was about to become famous.

Jackie was subdued. He held his hands in his lap. "Hi," I said, sliding into the seat beside him. He nodded.

Odessa lay twenty miles west of Midland, on Highway 80. Oil rigs and mobile home parks cluttered the tumbleweed-desert on either side of the road. We passed the Texan Drive-In, which showed X-rated movies. The marquee read *Fly Down Inside*. The sun had just set – orange streaked the sky near the sandy, flat horizon – and the feature had begun. The screen partially faced the highway; from the corner of my eye I could see a naked thigh the size of a diesel truck.

Mr. Waldrip stopped at Pinkie's Liquor and bought two bottles of Old Charter and some paper cups. He toasted his wife twice before we even left the parking lot.

Jackie looked out the window, at fences and cows.

Odessa was a blue-collar town – people there manufactured drilling equipment for the oil patch – whereas Midland was a banking center. I remember my father saying Odessa was a filthy city, full of toughs, bums, and thieves. He said he'd never live there.

The Waldrips, on the other hand, looked and felt more at home once we entered the "Big O." "I just love the Big O," said Jackie's mother.

Ace Records, the recording studio – a square, cinder-block building which I'm sure no longer stands – was located on a narrow corner, under a giant sign for Salem cigarettes. A red light glowed above the door. The place was locked tight.

Mrs. Waldrip insisted that I pull my drums out of the car and set them on the sidewalk.

"Honey, why don't we wait'll the man comes and opens the door?" asked Jackie's father.

"He'll be here any minute." She pinched Jackie's arm. "You ready to go?" He shrugged. "Gonna cut us a hit!" She poured herself some whiskey. "Top forty, coast to coast."

A gust of wind blew my crash cymbal over. It clattered on the sidewalk, frightening a cat from under a car across the street.

Handbills and hamburger wrappers blew against the Waldrip's red wagon. We waited for thirty minutes.

"Son of a bitch said he'd meet us here at seven-thirty," Jackie's mother said.

"When did you talk to him last?" her husband asked. He'd opened the second bottle of bourbon.

"Just this morning."

We waited another half hour.

"Screw it," said Jackie's father.

"But I want to sing my song!"

"Another night, honey. Let's go see the Weavers." He put his arm around his wife's shoulders and led her to the car. Jackie and I lifted my drums into the back seat. "Big baby," he whispered.

"What?" I said.

"Nothing."

We drove through neighborhoods where the lawns weren't mowed, where people left strings of Christmas lights in their eaves all year.

"Who are the Weavers?" I whispered to Jackie.

He shrugged.

Mr. Waldrip stopped the car in front of a small Spanish-style home made of brown brick. A power line buzzed over-head. A water tower, shiny in the moonlight, stood at the end of the street.

Joy Weaver, a thin woman with dark, stiff skin, hugged

Jackie's parents in the doorway. "I'll be durned, look what the cat dragged in," she said. Her light blond hair reminded me of the fiberglass insulation in the heating unit my father had installed last week at home.

"Earl here?" asked Mr. Waldrip.

"Ol' sourpuss is out playing cards."

"Well, he'll miss the party." Mr. Waldrip handed her the near-empty bottle of Old Charter.

"Sweetie, we can do better than that." Joy Weaver pulled two bottles of Jim Beam out of a cabinet underneath a bookshelf.

"We even brought live entertainment," Mr. Waldrip said, pointing to Jackie and me. "These boys is *hot!*"

Jackie scrunched into a chair by the television set. A velvet painting of Christ kissing a child hung above a hound's-tooth couch at the far end of the den. A marionette in a straw sombrero, gripping two silver pistols, dangled from the ceiling next to an ivy plant.

"You kids want a beer?" asked Joy Weaver.

"No," Jackie said. He seemed about to cry. His face was red.

"Sure, I'll try one," I said.

"David, get your drums," said Mrs. Waldrip. "Let's do my song for Joy."

"You wrote a song?"

"Hell yes, girl, I told you someday I was going to crawl out of this hole and be famous."

"I always knew it," Joy said. "I wish I had your talent."

"I wish I had her time," said Jackie's father. "Shit, *I* could write a song if all I did was sit home all day." I didn't know then, and I don't know now, what he did for a living.

"We oughta get Ida to sing. Have you ever heard Ida sing?" Joy said. "She does 'Bobby McGee' worlds better than that Joplin woman can."

"Where *is* Ida?" said Mr. Waldrip.

"I think she's back in her room, doing her homework. Ida! Ida Mae! We got company!"

I'd unloaded my drums by now. I stood by the couch, tightening the wing nuts on the hi-hat, testing the tom-tom's tone with the drum key.

A pretty young girl in jeans and a pullover sweater came into the room and sat down. Her brown hair was pulled tight into a ponytail. She had blue eyes.

"Jackie, what grade are you in?" Joy asked.

"Tenth," he mumbled.

"So's Ida. We oughta get you kids together more often."

Jackie chewed his guitar pick.

We ran through Mrs. Waldrip's song, then Joy asked us if we knew "Bobby McGee."

Jackie didn't say anything. Buoyed by the beer I said, "I could fake it."

"Mother, I don't want to sing," Ida told Joy.

"Baby, you're so much better than what's-her-name."

"No I'm not."

"Gravelly old voice – woman sounds like she's barfing in a cup. You make *sweet* sounds."

"David, count her into the song," Mrs. Waldrip said.

I hesitated, hands above the snare, sticks trembling. "No, Mother," Ida said. She looked directly at me.

"David, one, two, three – "

I tapped out a standard rock beat. Mrs. Waldrip glared at Jackie; he filled in the rhythm. Ida's cheeks turned red.

"She's a *pistol,*" Joy said. "Let's hear it, honey."

Ida's voice was so heartbreakingly wrong for the tune, I fell in love with her instantly. So did Jackie. We didn't speak about it then or later, but we'd both seen on each other's faces a desire to rescue this girl from her mother, to take her away someplace, somehow, on the back of a wild horse, maybe, where there weren't any parents or rock and roll records.

Ida sang about Bobby's body as though she were in church.

I felt ashamed for her in front of these people. I wanted to sit and hold her hand. Mr. Waldrip had his arm around Joy Weaver.

Ida broke off in the middle of the performance and ran to the kitchen. The Waldrips clapped. "Bravo, bravo," Joy said. She poured another round of bourbon.

I looked at Jackie. He didn't move. I stood, jammed my sticks into my back jeans pocket, and followed Ida into the kitchen. She was sitting at the table, opening a loaf of bread. "You want a peanut butter sandwich?" she said. Her eyes were wet and her face was still red.

"No thanks."

Jackie joined us. "You sing real well," he said.

Ida laughed, but kept her eyes on him. "No, really," he told her. He looked solemn and calm. Handsome. Sometimes his sullenness made him seem older than he was, centered and important. The impression lasted only a moment, as if he felt it wasn't his place in the world to be so assertive. He fumbled for something else to say.

"These people are nuts," I said.

Ida leaned away from Jackie. "God, *aren't* they?" She put her hand on my arm and we laughed.

"And the hits just keep on rollin'!" I crooned. Ida cracked up. She was so pretty. Jackie smiled. I could tell I'd hurt him by saying his folks were nuts. He'd trusted me not to say a word about them, ever.

Jackie and I didn't see Ida again after that night, but clearly, in his mind, I'd won her. My parents were angry when the Waldrips dropped me off at one A.M., banging and clattering my drums, and waking the neighbors. They wouldn't let me go to Jackie's house anymore; eventually, he stopped coming to rehearsals after school. Without him, the rest of the "Crystals" lost interest.

I went alone to finish our English project. The workers wouldn't talk to me as easily as they had with Jackie. I asked them about mariachi music and "La Paloma," one of my favorite Mexican songs. I told them I was a drummer. They stood in a nervous circle, spat tobacco in the sand, and looked at me as though I were a wolf.

Jackie never mentioned the project. I turned in the transcripts and we both got a C, with a note from the teacher, "This seems incomplete." For weeks afterwards, I felt bad about the workers, writing their stories when they so clearly didn't want me to. Eventually I understood that my real regret was Jackie. I hadn't meant to be cruel about his folks – just as I hadn't planned to anger Peggy Sue with my quarter – but I'd wanted

Ida's attention. I hadn't fully realized, until that night, how similar love and betrayal were, and how capable I was of both.

Months later, I heard from my father that most of the oil workers were undocumented. They'd been arrested and deported, and the drilling company closed.

———

In the next two years I saw Jackie only at marching practice. I'd wave to him from across the field. He'd nod, clutching his French horn like a shield. I never learned anything more about his parents, or what it was like for him at home. I joined another rock group in town and we earned a little money playing dances and parties. At the senior prom Jackie appeared with a date who looked remarkably like Ida Mae Weaver (it wasn't her). My band had been hired for the gig, and at the break Jackie told me, "You sound strong. Your wrists are a little stiff – seems to me you're not as limber as you used to be – but you're cooking."

I thought we might be friends again, but we were still so young, we believed we were exempt from time. Neither of us made another gesture, and when I left for college a few months later I lost track of him.

Several years after that, at a high school reunion, someone said they thought Jackie Waldrip was a wildcatter down around McCamey, but no one knew for sure. I drove by his old house when the reunion was over. The rodeo grounds and all the horses were gone. So were the shutters on the windows. A welder's truck was parked in the drive.

I sat in my car, remembering Jackie and Ida. In a way I'd abandoned them when I'd gone off to school, used my father's connections to position myself in life.

I hoped Ida Mae had prospered, but that night in her house, I hadn't glimpsed any reason to think she would. Options were scarce for a working-class woman in Odessa, Texas.

Two boys were wrestling now in Jackie's old yard, laughing, throwing grass. I recalled my twin ambitions of becoming a rock star, of losing myself in endless romantic affairs. They'd diminished, then disappeared, like the Pride of the Mustangs rounding a corner at the far end of a street.

I started my car and pulled away, watching the boys in my rearview, and with their image in my mind I can say now as I couldn't then: I loved Jackie. His absence from my life haunts me as Ida Mae did, though I'm also convinced that, given the time and place of our growing up, and our backgrounds, it was inevitable that we'd vanish from each other.

As for Ida — for years, even after I'd married, she was my physical model for the ideal woman, until, with time, her face became harder and harder to recall with any accuracy.

Yesterday, when Philip found my drums, he seemed reverential — toward the strange equipment, me. Here was a side of his dad he'd never known. But his awe soon passed. "I'm gonna be on MTV!" he shouted. He whacked the cymbals and the snare, drowning out the story I'd started to tell him about a pretty young girl I met one night, and the beat went on all day.

THE WOMAN IN THE OIL FIELD

On the west side of Dallas my grandmother, no longer beautiful, sits in a wheelchair in a Catholic nursing home. Her room is across the hall from a bathroom and there is one old man – like her, a resident of the place – who forgets to shut the door when he goes to use the john. My grandmother shouts at him and he looks up, startled; the nurses come to clean his urine off the floor. In a rage he steps into my grandmother's room but before he can say anything she raises her voice. "What are you sleeping with that shanty woman for?" she yells. She's confused him with my grandfather Bill, who (family legend has it) ran off with a prostitute, an "oil field woman," in the thirties. "She teases me," my grandmother says to the old man. "She comes to me at night and tells me I won't ever sleep with you again. Then she ties my bed to a gelding and he runs me around a field, fast and dizzy, and the whole time she's laughing. In the mornings when the women here bathe me she's outside my window and I try to hide my body but they won't let me. They want to show her what I've become. Do you want her to laugh at me? Am I repulsive to you now?" The nurses smile because she's mistaken the man, but she has a story to understand and it's the same one I heard in my mother's kitchen twenty years ago. Lately, on these hot summer Friday afternoons, trying to convince Grandma June that her husband Bill is dead, I've remembered the story and learned new ways to tell it. When I'm older and not the same man, I know I'll find another way, then another, until I've resolved it for myself.

I stop in and see June, regular as a city bus, on Monday and Friday mornings, and stay most of the day. Sometimes she knows I'm here, sometimes she doesn't. I've been back in Dallas now, out of work, for eight and a half months, ever since Boeing's Seattle plant laid me off with ninety-nine other machinists. When I called last fall to tell my folks about the pink slip, my mom said I should head back south. "It'd be a blessing if you could ease June's final days," she said. "I can't go to Dallas each time she gets to feeling blue – Exxon's bringing in a new well near Oklahoma City and they've got your father looking after it. Mother's asking for me but your daddy needs me here," she said. "Stay with her, Glen. We'll cover your expenses."

I thought it over for a day, then figured what the hell – beats hanging in the Seattle rain looking for jobs. Besides, though we'd never spent much time together, I'd always liked June. She was a straight talker. So I threw a pack of clothes into my Chevy and fastened a set of chains to my tires. I rumbled up the Rockies, dipped into the desert, and wound up in Texas again.

On Monday evenings now, when I leave June asleep, I hit the road and don't turn around until Friday. Six hundred, eight hundred miles a week just to get away from the sickrooms, the musty medicine smells of the Parkview Manor Nursing Home. Tumbleweeds blow across the highways, in all the little towns of West Texas. I remember these towns from my childhood, but I can't tell them apart anymore now that the damn franchises've moved in everywhere. Dairy Queens and Motel Sixes. HBO and Showtime blaring in people's houses, through the windows. On Friday afternoons, back in Dallas, I tell June I've sat with her all week. She doesn't know the difference if I'm here or away. "You remember yesterday?" I ask. "I read you the newspaper?" She has a favorite daily column, "The Winds of Time," by this local hack historian, Larry Kircheval. His articles always start, "Whatever happened to – ?" and tell the story of some boring old building or once-important citizen. He irritates the hell out of me, really bares his heart when he writes – "Look at *me*, how much I know, how much I *feel* about the past" – but June eats it up. I read her his stuff whenever I'm here. On Saturday mornings my folks call from Oklahoma City and say they've tried to reach me all week at my Dallas apartment – an efficiency with only a table and a single bed ("All we can afford for you right now," Dad says). "We must've just missed each other," I tell them. "I go out for ice cream a lot. It's turning hot here now . . ."

———

This afternoon two irritable old men, bound to their wheelchairs with thick silk straps, sit in the lobby of the Parkview Manor Nursing Home in front of the big-screen TV. An old cop movie in black-and-white: leering killers, screaming women. The actor's faces, flattened and pale against the lime green wall behind the screen, remind me of old photographs I've seen in the memory books here, on nightstands beside the beds.

A slow ceiling fan swirls dust motes across the lobby floor. Brown summer horseflies light on the old men's cotton sleeves. They're wearing yellow pajamas – standard Parkview dress – and leather slippers. They don't like each other: I can see that. Both are new arrivals here, never met before today, but while the movie hums at high volume these two guys're giving each other the glare. June's asleep; I've stepped into the lobby to stretch my legs, to get a Coke from the patio machine out front. As I'm sorting dimes I hear one old bird rasp at the other, "You son of a bitch," and suddenly they're both throwing punches. The rubber wheels of their chairs squeal against each other and scuff the red tile floor. These fellows're too weak to really hurt each other, but the nurses panic and glide them toward separate corners of the room. "Mr. Davis! Mr. Edwards!" shouts one of the nurse's aides. On the television screen a masked burglar jimmies a window.

Good for you, I think, watching the old men grimace and cough. Don't let the fire go out. (I swear I've heard – late at night, when only Nurse Simpson's on duty, Nurse Simpson who lets me stay if June's had a hard evening – I swear I've heard the sounds of sexual pleasure, whether from memory – a murmuring in sleep – or actual contact, I can't tell.)

I go to check on June. She's awake now, lying in bed, clutching her box of Kleenex. She's nearly blind; if she pats around on the sheet and can't find her Kleenex she cries. Her hands are tiny and clawlike, tight with arthritis. Sometimes, to exercise or just to pass the hours, she rolls and unrolls a ball of blue yarn.

I ask her if she wants some apple juice.

"Yes," she says.

I turn the crank at the end of the bed to raise her up; hold the cup, guide the straw into her mouth. Her teeth are gone.

"You tell him to talk to me," she says.

"Who?" I ask.

"Stubborn old man." She waves at a chair by the wall. "He's been sitting there all afternoon reading that damn paper and he won't talk to me." Her voice cracks. "Where's your whore today, old man? Off with someone else?"

I stroke the papery skin of her arms, offer more juice. She's ninety-two years old. Since Bill died she's had two other husbands (divorced one, outlived the other), six grandkids, and three careers (store owner, upholsterer, quilt-maker). But now, near the end of her life, it's this one incident – Bill and the oil field woman – that clogs her mind. She's been jealous for sixty years.

She sips her juice. Her head seems to clear. "Glen?" she says.

"I'm here."

"Bill's not really sitting in that chair, is he?"

"No, June."

"He's dead?"

"That's right."

"When?"

"When did he die? A long time ago – 1962 or '63, I think it was."

"I remember now. In a drunk tank."

"Yes."

Sunlight spreads, first bright then pale, through her peach-colored curtains. An air-conditioning vent above her bed flutters a poster taped loosely to the wall. Last week a Catholic church group, on their regular visit, left these posters in all the rooms: a little girl hugging a kitten. The caption reads, "I Know I'm Special – God Don't Make No Junk."

"Can I get you something else, June?"

"French fries."

"All that grease?"

"Get me some goddamn French fries!"

I don't know how she chews the silly things with just her gums, but she does. "All right," I say. "I'll be back."

I drive a few blocks to a Burger King. The streets here on the west side're lined with sexy new cigarette ads – enormous, rolling breasts filling billboards. I lift my foot off the gas pedal and coast in my lane, staring, more lonely than horny, at these huge women floating like helium balloons over the start-stop traffic. By the time I return to the rest home the sun's set. The red light from the Coke machine on the patio pours through June's window. She's sitting up in bed, in the near-dark, twining yarn. From the big-screen TV canned laughter echoes down the hall. The curtains rustle, from the air vent. June's squinting, trying to catch the movement. I don't know how much she can see. She shushes me. "That whore is there at the window," she whispers. I dangle a French fry under her nose. "She's laughing," June says. "Listen."

Nurse Simpson pokes her head into the room, says, "How we doing?"

June says, "Bitch."

"We're fine," I tell the nurse. "But maybe I'd better stay here tonight."

She nods. "I'll bring the cot," she says.

———

I first heard about June's whore late one night in my mother's kitchen. I was twelve. Mother suspected my sixteen-year-old sister was in trouble, smoking dope, driving into dark fields with boys in dirty pants. "When I was her age I could've wound up that way," Mom said. "It would've been easy. Now your sister."

"What way do you mean?" I asked.

She told me the story then: "When she was young, your Grandma June was very beautiful. My father's a fortunate man to've touched her. He was an oil worker in the East Texas fields, and not too smart, not too good or bad. At Christmas he drove home to Dallas bringing us store-wrapped gifts, and slept with us in the house. Your grandmother kept him busy with the vegetables for dinner or the furnace or anything else that needed looking after. At night he combed her blond hair and when he got through his hands seemed to take on her fair color and not the deep black they always seemed to be. But that's me, you know, because I know his hands weren't black. He washed the oil off – I never even saw crude oil – but he worked in the fields and I see him now, dark, in my mind.

"The woman who took him from us wasn't beautiful like your grandmother but she slept in the shanties by the fields and sooner or later he found her, like they all did I suppose, all the men who worked in the East Texas fields. It wasn't uncommon to see women strapping on their shoes at night and heading for the fields because there was money to make and they knew it. So he found her sooner or later. If he came home at Christmas he didn't work around the house anymore. Then he didn't come at all and he was with her, we knew. My brother Bud was old enough to take care of us now so he said, 'Don't worry,' but I knew he'd be lost, like Daddy. The fields were the only place for him to go."

One night, driving home for the weekend, Bud ran his car

off the road two miles south of a rig he'd been roughnecking. He never regained consciousness, Mother said.

"Did he ever see your father?" I asked her.

"No, and he didn't meet a woman of his own. He wasn't the type to take up with that sort, and anyway we'd heard the shanty woman was dead by now, killed by some old boy who didn't want to pay for her. They found her half-burned in the Mayberry Field, dress off, doused with gas."

"Whatever happened to Grandfather Bill?" I asked.

"We heard about him, sick and dying, in a Kilgore clinic years later." My mother rubbed her throat; she'd gone dry. As in many family stories, the initial point had been lost in the telling. I never understood her fear about becoming the kind of woman she'd described. Maybe she'd been tempted to follow the oil workers herself when she was young, to raise money for June who'd had to scramble for cash after Bill disappeared. In fact, my mother didn't leave home until she met my father – who also eventually wound up in the fields. (My sister, more level-headed than Mother ever gave her credit for being, turned out fine. She's married now and living in Houston.)

That night, twenty years ago, sitting with me in her kitchen, my mother laughed sadly. "I don't know what's so damned attractive about the oil fields, but every man in my life has been drawn to them."

I remember thinking, Not me. I won't be trapped by that hard-packed Texas ground.

"Bud was such a good kid," she said. "There was no need for it, no need for it at all . . . when he ran his car off the road, people said the marks looked like he'd swerved to miss something, but there weren't any tracks in the dirt."

At twelve, I was already familiar enough with my mother's grim tales to know they usually ended in guilt or remorse. I knew what Bud had swerved to miss on the road that night. I knew why Mother worried about my father when he worked late. The oil field woman would haunt my family from now on.

My father's a quiet man, and shy, and even if the shanties still stood during his wildcatting days he wouldn't have gone to them for the world. But the Mayberry Woman, as she was known in the fields, came to the oil workers now, the way she'd come to Bud and stood like fog in the middle of the road. She didn't say why she came. Maybe she was looking for her money, though what could it mean to her now?

In 1963 my father moved up in the small oil company he worked for. He stopped going to the fields. He bought an air-conditioner and a new car for us, and paid off the mortgage on June's Dallas home. In the evenings we watched television. Dad said the country would never recover from Oswald's rifle in the window. No one told me stories at night to put me to bed. My mother fretted about my sister, my father read the paper. In time, I began to realize it was up to me: I'd been given a version of a story, though I was too young to know how to tell it.

———

For a long time the story stayed inside me. When I was a little older (but still too young to know how to begin) I scared myself with it. Watching meteors one dusk in a mesquite-ridden field I had the sense that the Mayberry Woman was just behind a bush. I wouldn't go to her. A few yards away, on the highway, diesel trucks signaled one another with their horns. I hoped she'd know the drivers were stronger men than I was, full of hard little pills to keep them awake. They'd give her more of whatever it was she was looking for than I could. Presently a jeep loaded with Mexican boys pulled up to the edge of the field. The sky had turned coal black. A spotlight in the back of the jeep flashed on and the boys fired at cottontail rabbits cowering in the mesquite. I sank into myself. The shots didn't come my way. As they hunted the boys sang a story of their own:

La pena y la que no es pena; ay llorona
Todo es pena para mi.

The story was similar to mine: an airy woman, damp with sweat and talcum and cheap perfume, walked the streets of a Mexican town, touching the faces of children, seducing men from the taverns, lying with them in the back seats of rusted cars.

The hunters laughed and didn't even want the dead rabbits. I imagined that, years from now, after they'd forgotten this night, they'd remember the story they were singing. *La Llorona* was more embedded in their minds than the spotlight and the guns, and I felt a kind of kinship with them.

This morning I overhear two nurses in the hall, whispering about me. One says, "It's awful the way he leaves his grandma each week, then sneaks back and tells her he's been here the whole time."

"She doesn't know one way or the other. Her poor old noodle just comes and goes," the second woman says.

"Still, he oughtn't to lie to her that way."

Last night a woman died in the room next to June's. It was the first time I'd ever heard a death rattle. Her last breaths came gurgling out of her throat like water draining in a sink. Nurse Simpson cleared her out of her bed, an ambulance pulled up outside the building's back entrance, and that was it.

Now June's clutching and unclutching a Kleenex in her hand. I open the curtains to let in the light. The two nurses who've been whispering enter the room with a pill cart. Tiny color snapshots of all the Parkview residents have been arranged in rows on the tray, next to little paper cups full of capsules and pills. Orange, red, yellow, green. One of the nurses finds June's photo, picks up her cup. Her pills are gray. "Get those things away from me," June says, covering her mouth with the Kleenex.

"Junie, now, be a good girl – "

"Trying to poison me with that crap."

The nurse forces the pills into June's mouth with quick sips of juice. "Ought to try to walk a little today," she says, squeezing June's feet. "Work your legs some."

"I walked for ninety years. Leave me alone," June says.

The nurse's white blouse is spotted with large yellow stains. Someone's breakfast. She gives me a hurried look, and I know she's the one who disapproves of me.

"Thank you," I say as she replaces June's cup on the tray.

The pills always knock June out. While she sleeps I flip through a stack of Kodak prints my mother sent us last week. Family snapshots. A picture of Mom in her high school cheerleading outfit; her graduation portrait. June pruning roses in her yard. There aren't any pictures of Bill. June destroyed them all years ago, when he left.

An alarm bell rings in the lobby. I go to see what's happened. Mr. Edwards has tried to escape. He's rammed open the back door, the ambulance entrance, with his wheelchair. He has an old fedora on his head and a blue sweater draped across his shoulders; otherwise he's naked. Briefly, I find myself rooting for him but the nurses catch him as he rounds the patio. "Sons of bitches!" he shouts, spurring his chair like a pony.

At lunch the Soup of the Day smells like mercurochrome. June won't eat it. I bring her a ham and cheese sandwich from Burger King. She's lucid and calm. "Where's your wife, Glen? Didn't you get married?" she says.

The question catches me off guard. "No. Well, yes."

"Shoot, boy." She cackles then coughs. "Are you in or out?"

"We split up about a year ago," I tell her. "She's in New Mexico now." Marge and I only lived together for a few months in a small apartment near Puget Sound. Mom had told June we were married; she wouldn't have understood the kind of loose arrangement we had.

"What was the problem?" June asks.

"I don't know. I didn't make enough money to suit her."

"What is it you do?"

"I'm a welder."

"That's right, that's right. Making airplanes."

"You want these fries?"

She holds out her hand. "I never understood why you moved way the hell up there, anyway. What's wrong with Texas?"

"Nothing's wrong with Texas. I just didn't want to work in the oil fields." I brush a horsefly off the sandwich paper. "I heard it was pretty out west, so I went."

"There's worse jobs than the oil fields," June says.

I laugh. "Sure there are. It's just – "

"What?"

"I don't know, June, it seemed kind of aimless to me. Bill, Bud, even Dad. Moving around from patch to patch . . ."

"Are you better off making airplanes?"

"No." I squeeze her hand. "Not really. You want the rest of this?"

"Tastes like tar." She says she's tired. I tell her I'm going to run into town, but I'll be back this evening. I drive to my apartment and pack a handful of clothes.

The girls on Cedar Springs Boulevard don't want to work for their money. I've asked before – every damn night when I first got to town and felt so low. Ten minutes, sixty bucks.

Before I hit the road I stop at Ojeda's on Cedar Springs and order a taco. A pug-nosed girl, fourteen or fifteen, in red heels and a black jacket, taps the restaurant window. Long purple nails. I shake my head, ladle salsa onto my plate. "I love you," she mouths through the glass. I hold up three fingers. "Thirty bucks," I say. She laughs and moves down the walk, swaying like a dancer.

I've often wondered what caught Bill's eye in the oil field, when the shanty woman first showed up. A twist of hips, a toss of the head?

I eat and read the paper. Today Kircheval's column – June's favorite – starts, "Years ago, on a tall building in downtown Dallas, the Mobil Oil Company erected a revolving red Pegasus, rearing and about to take flight. The city's preservation committee protects the sign now because Mobil abandoned the flying horse as its trademark over a decade ago."

Kircheval's sad that few old Dallasites recall the name of the company that lifted the sign onto the building, and fewer still remember the original legend of Pegasus.

"So many losses," he goes on. "Like Jack Ruby's bar – can anyone find its old spot? A few people point out the grassy knoll, but that's all. No one talks about it. No one talks about the sky we can't see behind the streetlights." I imagine him, poor sentimental bastard, sitting at a scratched wooden desk in the newspaper office, surrounded by World War Two press photos of Ernie Pyle ("Now *there* was a journalist!").

"Have we forgotten about the Dipper scooping down out of the north?" he asks. "Have we forgotten falling stars and all the things that used to scare us?"

I-20 West through Ft. Worth, Abilene, Big Spring, Mid-land-Odessa, runs – a straight shot – past refineries and rigs. Flames breathe fiercely out of steel-plated towers and drums; around the processing plants the air smells flat, like warm asparagus.

Last month, on one of my escape-runs, I filled out job applications with Exxon and Arco. As much as I'd hate to give myself to Oil, to fasten my gaze on the ground, I realize I'll need someplace to go when June passes on.

When I was a kid I wanted to ride the pumps in the fields. They bucked up and down like the wild-maned rodeo broncos I saw on TV, or like coin-operated horses in front of the dime stores Mama used to shop.

This afternoon thick blue thunderheads mass together in the east. A faint smell of rain mingles with sand in the air. I stop in Abilene for a DQ Dude and some onion rings. The Dairy Queen is overrun with high school majorettes. They're wearing green and yellow uniforms and hats with plumes. Big, strapping Texas girls: I'm reminded of the picture of my mother when she was a cheerleader.

Back on the highway I pass the ripped screens of drive-in movie theaters, closed for years. Actors' faces, wide as tractors, used to kiss and sing here, floating above me like cloud-banks on the horizon.

The rain lets go as I pass the Big Spring cutoff. Semis swish by me, kicking up spray and dust. I stop for gas, a couple of cold Coors. At Midland I turn west toward New Mexico. Watching my blinker flash green, I realize what I'm doing. All these lonely trips I've taken, all the times I've strayed from Dallas – practice runs. For thousands of miles, back and forth through veils of Texas dust, I've been working up my nerve.

Marge and I haven't spoken in nearly a year, since she took up with Calvin Reynolds. Cal's an old Boeing buddy of mine, an engineer. After the big layoffs in Seattle he got a job at one of the labs in Los Alamos, and talked Marge into going with him. By then she and I were pretty well finished anyway.

The beer's made me sleepy so I check into a cinder-block

motel – The Rayola – just outside of Monahans. A rusty sign above the office door shows a cowboy in pajamas and a night-cap sitting up in bed, still wearing his boots, twirling a lariat.

For a while I sit smoking, staring at David Letterman and the tan brick wall of my room. I drop ashes into a motel glass. It was wrapped in clear plastic when I first picked it up, but now I notice a lipstick stain on its rim. I lie awake, listening to rain wash the streets and tap my curtained window.

———

West of Odessa there used to be a meteor crater. I remember seeing it as a kid: a rock bowl, perfectly smooth, carved deep into the planet. Now it's filled nearly to the lip with dirt and old hamburger wrappers. The oil boom's over in this part of Texas – the parks are overgrown, the rigs're left standing just for show. Ghost towns. Most of the fields are depleted. If you pump oil out of the earth too fast, my father told me once, the salt domes under the soil will collapse, and sinkholes open in the land, spreading through weeded lots, rippling under high-ways, shattering concrete. In the past, whole communities have disappeared, he said. Swing sets, dress shops, signs . . .

———

Roswell, New Mexico. I push open the phone booth door, slip a quarter out of my pocket. Jet planes hurtle across the sky, into or out of a nearby Air Force base. From the booth I watch their vapor trails and wonder if I welded any of that sun-warmed metal.

For a moment, as I grip the receiver, I want to free myself like a hawk, like a flying horse, from the ground's heavy pull.

Cal answers the phone. I haven't thought of what to say to him, so I just ask for Marge.

"Glen?" he says.

"Yeah. It's me."

He takes a breath. He doesn't know what to say either. "Hold on a minute," he tells me. "I'll see if she's here."

I watch a man in a car dealership across the street from the booth try to sell a young couple a used Toyota.

Marge comes on the line with a fake cheery voice. "Glen! How the hell are you?"

"Okay." I tell her about June. "I'm living in Dallas now."

"So you're sightseeing?"

"I thought I'd come see you. I miss you."

"Oh," she says. I can picture her lips – the way they pucker when she talks. I can picture the kind of dress she's wearing, baggy and bright. Every day I've seen her in my mind the way June glimpses, everywhere she looks, the woman in the oil field. "I don't know, Glen, it's kind of a loopy time around here – Cal's daughter Lynn is coming for a visit tomorrow. I'm kind of nervous, you know, we've never met before. There's some good movies in town we can take her to. And we've stocked up on Spaghetti-Os. She loves Spaghetti-Os."

The familiar ring of Marge's voice makes me prickly and hot, but her cool tone – she's closing me out even as she's drawing me back in – infuriates. I rub the booth glass with the flat of my thumb, pressing harder with each long stroke.

Lenny, Jack, Cal: she sang the names like a nursery rhyme the night I heard I was fired. I came home weary from the plant, ready to pick a fight, got drunk, asked her who she'd been sleeping with since we'd moved in together. We both knew how matters stood. "What about you?" she said.

Shirley, Florence, Joy . . .

I thought I was ready for whatever hard things Marge had to tell me that night, but you're never really prepared for the full, fat weight of jealousy.

"Anyway, I hope your grandma gets better," she tells me now on the phone.

"She won't get better. She's old," I say.

"Right."

"You still don't listen, baby."

"Glen – "

"Did you keep that little T-shirt, the one I bought you on the coast? With the whales on it? I bet Cal likes it, right?"

"Glen, don't start."

"Okay. So . . ."

"I better go. Cal'll need his lunch."

"Fuck him," I say.

"I'm going to go now, Glen."

"You too." I hang up the phone. The sound barrier cracks. Jets thunder over the desert.

On Friday afternoon the rest home is quiet. Water trickles inside a brown plastic air-conditioner wedged into a window by the back door where the ambulance came again this morning. Mr. Davis.

The nurses play Hearts or Spades at the main desk in the lobby.

June's been sleeping. Now she blinks her eyes. "Glen?"

"I'm here, June."

"Where've you been?"

"By your bed. All afternoon."

"What about yesterday?"

"Don't you remember?"

"No." She sits up. I fluff her pillows. "Do you have the paper?" she asks. "Read me old what's-his-name."

Today Kircheval shares with his readers the complete history of Ft. Worth's sewage system. I glance at the column, hesitate, then say, "He's not in the paper today, June. Must be on vacation."

"I need a story," she says. "Expect me to *lie* here all day, just worrying and waiting for that woman to show, with nothing else on my mind – "

"I've got a story, June." I pull my chair up close to the bed. "A better story than Kircheval could tell. Want to hear it?"

"What's it about?"

"I think it's about . . ." I stare at the poster on her wall, the little girl hugging the kitten. I feel silly that a gooey scene like this can move me, the way Kircheval touches a nerve in June, but it does. "I think it's about redemption."

June licks her dry lips. "I don't like religious stories."

"No no, this isn't like that." I get her a glass of water. "This one's about a woman in an oil field, but she was a good woman, June, not like the ladies you've heard of."

"A good woman?"

"A very good woman. Men came to her – "

"*Bet* they did."

" – and she'd turn them away. Said, 'You got a wife and kids back home. Don't mess with that.' "

"Who *is* this woman?"

"She'd bring folks together again, folks who'd lied to each other and said hurtful things. Told the ladies at home, 'Your man's brave in the fields, works hard all day, so don't you bad-mouth him for not being around.' And she'd tell the men stories of their women, how they sacrificed raising the children, but how nice and bright they all were, how much they all missed him, and the men'd smile and watch oil gush out of the ground – "

"Damned old oil, ruined *everybody's* life . . .," June says.

"No, June, the oil was good. Built factories and schools . . . this lady I'm telling you about, the Mayberry Woman they called her – "

"Mayberry? That ain't the story."

"It is, June."

"She was a bad woman. Awful old bitch."

"No, she was good. Listen. *Listen.* She used to bathe in oil, in a solid gold tub with these lion-claw feet made of brass, see? Rubbed thick crude on her arms like she was lathering in riches. Then she bottled up her fortune and shared it with everyone in Texas, men and women both."

June's breathing evenly now. Her hands lie still on her tissues.

"See, it's all right, June," I say. "It's always been all right, if you remember it this way."

The parking lot fills with noise. A Catholic youth group – eight ten-year-old girls with their mothers – bursts into the nursing home, giggling and shouting. The girls are carrying bunny rabbits – "fuzzy little friends for our friends here at the home," one says. They dump the rabbits into the laps of three or four women in wheelchairs. "Is it Easter?" a deaf old woman asks.

"No," the tallest mother says. She seems to be in charge. "We thought you'd like to pet them."

"Is it Christmas?"

Mr. Edwards glares at the bunnies as though he'd like to kill them.

I offer to wheel June into the lobby so she can feel the soft fur, but she doesn't want to. She smells like the sweet roll she had for breakfast. The air from her window cools us, rattles the newspaper; its sections lie scattered in a chair.

Her eyes cloud up, like marbles. I can see her mind's about to gallop off to the East Texas fields. She sleeps for a while. I sit and wonder where to head next Friday. New Mexico's out. West Texas has changed. Kansas, maybe, up through Oklahoma. *Boomer Sooner . . .*

When June wakes she tries to convince me that the shanty woman has murdered Bill and buried him here at the home.

"Where?" I say.

"On the patio. By the Coke machine."

"Would you like Nurse Simpson to check for you?"

"Bitch won't tell me."

"Why not?"

"She was sleeping with him, too."

"Nurse Simpson? I don't think she's Bill's type."

"Don't kid yourself," June says. "They're *all* his type."

She pounds around on the sheet for her Kleenex. When I give her the box she won't let go of my hand. The room's grown dark. Outside, sparrows squabble with a blue jay for space in a flowering plum tree.

"I should've killed him myself," June mutters. "Day he told me he's leaving . . ."

Her hand begins to tremble in mine. "Shhh," I say.

"Don't shush me, old man. Just get out of this house."

She tries to shove me away. In the shadows I watch her face and think none of us ever recovers from the first time we listen to someone else's sadness. We spend our lives refuting or repeating, trying to come to terms with the tales we've heard.

June looks at me. She pulls a wad of Kleenex from her box. "She's out there," she says, knotting the tissues. "She's out there waiting for me."

I say, "I know, June. But we don't have to go to her just yet." I smooth her hair and tell her again my story of the woman in the oil field.

FOUR A.M.

He rises at 4:43. Worried, worried. From his freezer he pulls an El Patio cheese and onion enchilada dinner with rice and refried beans. Since turning fifty he's had this meal each morning for breakfast: a quick-starter with after-burn to get him through the day. He reads the ingredients on the box. Zinc oxide, maltodextrin, sodium acid pyrophosphate, thiamine mononitrate, apocarotenal. These horrors are bound to kill him. He frowns, then happily preheats the oven, anticipating the sloppy, searing taste.

In the hallway he passes framed photos of his family on the walls. His grandfather, in the simpler first half of the century, only had to worry about a tree and that old swaybacked mule in his East Texas field, he thinks. Lucky man.

On his desk, official pleas from UNICEF, Amnesty International, PEN, the Union of Concerned Scientists to lend his famous name to their needs. He does, daily.

The oven timer rings. He cracks the seal on a bottle of cheap white wine, pours a tad in a coffee cup, lights a Camel, peppers his steaming enchiladas. It is 5:30. In the streets below his apartment window, buses lurch through the first green light of day, hunting the briefcase crowd, joggers in bright yellow shorts chase the chilly fur of their breath. He admires these adventurers who keep the city running, and on time. He toasts them with his vinegary wine.

This dawn, his task seems sadder than usual. *I'm weary. Have I lost another step? Damn booze.* But of course he'll stick till the end. Silence must be prodded at every turn – both the moral imagination and the cozy, known universe stretch thereby – so he lifts his pen and pokes reticence right in the belly, spilling a bundle of words.

First, a letter to General Wojciech Jaruzelski calling for an end to martial law, the release of imprisoned artists, educators, labor leaders and students, and a speedy restoration of basic human rights in Poland. He signs his name under the auspices of the Aspen Institute for Humanistic Studies, which has asked for his participation in this matter.

Next, a note to the American Library Association protesting the handiwork of a librarian in the Caldwell Parish Library in Louisiana. She has hand-painted diapers on the illustrations of Mickey, the naked little hero in Maurice Sendak's popular children's book *In the Night Kitchen,* on the grounds that the library's patrons might object to the nudity.

This second bit of business he takes as seriously as the first. The world does not distinguish between Evil and simple malfeasance, and one does well to heed the world.

In the afternoon he walks to the market on West Eleventh. Jalapeños, cigarettes, Scotch. Ground beef – the veal is too expensive. He'll make a pot of chili, freeze some for later. As he climbs back up the stairs inside his building he feels a pain in his lower abdomen. He stops to rest on a landing next to a neighbor kid's broken bike.

In his apartment he clicks on his radio. In a few minutes, at five, "Jazz Today" will start. He decides it's not too early for his first evening drink. In the courtyard below, behind his building, which he can see from his kitchen window, a man and a woman embrace, oblivious to sirens from somewhere, he guesses, in mid-Manhattan.

———

He puts his faith in things that don't quite work. Politics. Spiritual quests. His thirty-year-old apartment.

In his kitchen, while chopping peppers for the chili, he notices the ceiling is so badly cracked it appears to be leaving the wall. His landlord is harder to reach than the President. He wonders if he can spackle the gaps and let it go at that. In his twenties and thirties he was a pretty good handyman. He even built a harpsichord once, for the fun of using tools. He couldn't play it.

In Catholic school, when he was ten, the Jesuits steered him from his interest in music to the "higher discipline" of philosophy. He'd wanted to be a jazz drummer. Music was fine, they said, but God was in Ideas. After years of pleasurable exposure to both metaphysical ideas and live musical performances, he believes it takes a lot more discipline to be a drummer than to be a philosopher. Any fool can prattle on about the soul. Paradiddles are divine.

On the other hand, the Holy Ghost is the meanest cat he knows. A messy concept, the Holy Ghost, hard to pin down. It refuses to sit still on the specimen board. He prefers things messy – food, relationships, art. The too-tidy, the all-in-place are as stiff and unhappy as plastic. The ragged is much more human, he thinks, the never-finished nearly sublime!

Once, in a sidewalk tapas bar in the great city of Barcelona, a waiter gave him and his fellow Americans a stack of waxy napkins and said, in Catalan, "Just toss them on the ground when you're done." His companions, fastidious New Yorkers, tasted the olives and shrimp one by one, never mixing the dishes, carefully piled their napkins by their plates. Later, the waiter passed the table and, with a mighty sweep of his arm, knocked most of the paper into the street; it swirled with unruly pigeons high above a nearby cathedral, dipped and dodged between black cabs with the madness of confetti at a wedding. Few gestures he has seen in this world have delighted him as much.

After a bowl of his four-alarm chili he sets about, once more, the messy business of the planet: a piece for the op-ed page of the *Times,* which is running this month a series of guest columns by artists discussing their personal political fears. Which of the poisons to choose? The public seems tired, just now, of the large, perennial topics (refugees, famine). Contributions to national aid agencies declined last quarter. As every parent knows, at a certain point in the lesson the child shuts down and doesn't hear another word. He picks an old standby, an ongoing scandal but one that hasn't been in the news much lately – questionable payments by the aerospace industry to several U.S. senators. A call to action, effective education – the kind that gets results – is always a matter of timing. Success is fleeting. The issue is jacklighted then lost until some worried person at four A.M. notices nothing's changed.

He remembers his son, years ago, learning to ride a bike. One day, perfect execution; cries and crashes the next. Teaching is a hopeless process, full of hope. He believes in it, though often it leads only to sleepless dawns.

He walks to the market, he walks to museums. Like the great *flaneurs* of history – Baudelaire, Breton, Cornell – he is a connoisseur of the *merveilleux* in the ordinary. He understands that Broadway, Lexington, Fifth, in the swift march of their trades, are rich sites of libidinal possibility. He is simultaneously excited and terrified in a crowd, sprouting desire, tendrils of lust in all directions – that pushy redhead wrestling the Scribners' sacks, those slender brunettes in the cab – but the poor flesh can only hold so much, his heart will explode, so he dips into a neighborhood bar for refreshment and rest.

In the leather seat trimmed with warm applewood, he recalls three lines from the published excerpts of Joseph Cornell's diary: "Into the city . . . the buoyant feeling aroused by the buildings in their quiet uptown setting . . . an abstract feeling of geography and voyaging. . . ."

He downs his friendly drink then sets out again, past glum storefront mannequins, handshakes and shouts, paupers and dog shit and mint. Mint? Yes, a faint whiff from somewhere, around the corner, beyond the tail-exhaust of that speeding pizza truck. A miracle in a flux of commodities.

Was it Wittgenstein who spoke of the senses as ghosts in the night, glowing with weak whitish light? The city always strikes him this way, even in the flush of day. A sourceless luminous spirit, ever-moving, warping and woofing with his own inner needs.

A sculpture show at the MOMA. Giacometti's *Palace at Four A.M.*, crude yet elegant spires suggesting an empty castle where the king paces alone. Giacometti had in mind, while fashioning this piece, a lost lover, or so the story goes. In the museum's spiffy restaurant, still riding the artist's shapes in his mind, he recalls a recent phone talk with his son down in Texas. "Hey Dad, hired any topless canvas-stretchers yet?" Robert is grown now, married. A painter, like his father. *I tried to talk him out of it. I was a light-handed monarch, with simple expectations.*

"No. My cock dropped off at Lent."

"Seriously, Dad, are you dating? You're not too old."

"Thank you very much. Now if you'll excuse me I have to get my ankles realigned. Past a certain age, you know, they slip – "

"I'm sorry. I just thought you'd want to get out. Any more pains in the belly?"

"No." A lie. Accompanied now by nosebleeds.

"I'll call again next week."

Robert never forgave him for the divorce, but his concern, so many hard years later, is touching. First wife, second wife. One's in Europe now, one's in the grave, poor Ruth. He really did try to love them both, each in her turn. He really did fail. The palace has been empty for more than a decade.

In the food line, a young East Indian woman in a red halter dress, waiting for a slice of quiche, gives him a smile then moves on. Silently, with a moderately priced chardonnay, he toasts life's simple ecstacies.

Back on the street – chillier now, snow expected tonight – he's approached by a man he doesn't want to see, a fellow painter named Phillip, who shares his gallery. Phillip once challenged his remark that conceptual art is too easy. They'd been debating Robert Morris's *Box With the Sound of Its Own Making*, a nine-inch walnut cube containing a tape recorder which played, over and over, the hammering and sawing of its construction. The effect was of an artist trapped by his own artifact, sealed from the world – too neat, and he'd said so. "Besides, it's a one-joke piece."

Phillip disagreed. "I know, I know, you're active in all these international organizations, and you think art should be morally engaged."

"I didn't say it wasn't morally engaged. I said it was too neat."

Phillip, in a bright yellow muffler, is pumping his hand now in front of the musuem. "What are you doing tonight?" he says.

He mentions the follow-up letter to Poland.

Phillip doesn't hear. "I know. *Nothing* – how could you? The city's dead this time of year. Come on over to my place. Kenneth and Jane'll be there. We could play a little poker."

He sighs. Phillip seems to have a better time than he does.

The man looks genuinely crushed when he says he'll take a rain check. He should socialize. He knows he's losing touch with his friends, and he's surprised he doesn't worry about it more than he does.

"How's your work?"

He shrugs.

"Listen, I've been meaning to tell you, I think old Jansen" – their dealer – "is screwing us. I mean, I know the market's depressed, but come on! Kenneth and Jane and I want a showdown. Maybe next week. Are you with us? We're going to talk about it tonight."

"Some other time, Phillip, thanks."

Phillip's dark little mouth twists with disappointment. He tightens his muffler, nods then walks away.

Shuffling home, he remembers the streets at the height of the war: "Angry Arts Week" in '67. Poets moved in caravans shouting their outraged lyrics; postering brigades plastered windows with *Guernica*-like lithographs. Town Hall, he recalls, sponsored a conductorless performance of *The Eroica*, to symbolize the individual's responsibility for the brutality in Vietnam.

The Collage of Indignation, his own project with over a hundred other artists, was a "wailing wall," according to one critic, "alienated and homeless in style, embattled in content." Its contents – ugly, sordid and beautiful, as befits a cry of conscience – included a coil of barbed wire, a draft card and a rusty metal slab engraved with the words "Johnson is a Murderer." His spine tingles with the memory of its textures, its dangerous hues.

He thinks fondly of the heroes of the day. Meredith Monk. Her "dance protest" for draft-age boys. Alan Alda, Ruby Dee, John Henry Faulk and their "Broadway Dissents." Grace Paley, Donald Barthelme, Philip Roth.

Such imagination! And such false, fragile hopes, believing the pictures they made, the songs they sang could heal the planet's cancer. He doesn't see his buddies from that era any more. Most stopped singing. Others lost their minds.

He feels a marrow-chill, a lonely burst. Perhaps he should have accepted Phillip's invitation, after all. Jane is a good-looking woman, well-disposed toward him. Maybe he could charm her into . . .

A twinge in the throat. His nose is bleeding, damn it. He doesn't have a Kleenex. He wipes the blood on his hand, scrabbles in his pocket for his keys. In the stairwell the neighbor kid is moving her bike. "My daddy's going to fix the spokes," she says. The bike is too heavy for her; he helps her carry it to the next landing, all the while trying to stanch the stream from his nose. The child smiles at him, broadly. "Thanks."

"No problem."

"Are you okay?"

"Fine." This is still a world worth preserving, he thinks,

though – as he'd like to say to the girl – we must never stop arguing with it for the general improvement of its behavior and health.

He bloodies two handkerchiefs, cleaning his face. His favorite shirt's spotted red. Leftover chili. It's just as well he didn't ask Jane to come by.

"Jazz Today" is featuring *The Matterhorn Suite in Four Movements* by the Louie Bellson Drum Explosion. A whip-crack of golden cornets, then softer, slower, the purr of the bass, the slide of the hi-hat, smooth as K-Y Jelly. He saw Louie Bellson once, in the village. Working hard at the Vanguard. The memory is so pleasant he laughs out loud.

Later, his head hurts so he kisses the drums goodbye and searches through his records for harpsichord tunes. Something sacred and soothing. Is anything more sacred than the lambent strains of a harpsichord? He used to have an Igor Kipnis collection – or did he give it to a friend? He used to buy music, prints for his walls. He used to see movies. He remembers the title of a particularly gripping film, *The Onion Field,* but the story's a blank to him now, the actors unknown. His life is getting leaner. The cupboard bare. When did this start? How did it happen? He feels vaguely upset about it, but not enough to change anything. At least not tonight.

Before returning to his letters he clears a little space on his desk, finds, by coincidence, an old Xerox of a cablegram he'd sent Brezhnev in '74, when Solzhenitsyn was arrested. He remembers, two years later on an exchange tour, smuggling a packet of erotic lithographs by a banned artist out of Moscow. He feels a breath of nostalgia, the flush of success, enough to get him through the evening. He certainly would like some harpsichord music, though. For company he punches Channel Five. A man in a bad toupee leaps into a car from the roof of a bank. He punches it off.

He believes he smells Vietnamese cooking through the floor. The apartment below? Who lives there now? Probably just an aftershock of the day's thoughts. When he thinks of the war now, it seems to him a faraway, dissonant chord.

Someone shouts in the street. The first snow falls. He doesn't sleep well. At midnight, he's in the bathroom, throwing up his chili. In the toilet he sees a spot of blood. He lights a Camel, pours himself a Scotch.

———

He dreams of East Texas. His grandfather had a windmill that wouldn't move, even in a gale. The bolts were rusted fast. He'd sit with the old man and his gimpy mule all day, watching the sun course through the sky. The ranch's failure didn't much trouble the family. Or the mule. He admired his grandfather, immodestly: an eminently practical man with a natural gift for metaphor. "Nowadays," he said, "I don't worry about which way the wind blows."

———

Four A.M.: the hour of shuttered storefronts, vacant fire escapes. Sweats and chills. From his window he sees teens on the street, siphoning gas from a parked VW van. Sees smoke by the river. Hears a man and a woman through the wall – perhaps the couple he'd seen embracing in the courtyard a day or so ago. He pulls an El Patio from his freezer.

———

"How long have you been bleeding?" The doctor is stern with him, eavesdrops longer than usual on his heart and lungs (what *are* they gossiping about in there?). Taps his back, his chest, his throat. Orders tests. Endless tests. Forgoes the diet speech, the booze speech, the smokes speech. What's the point, now? The Holy Ghost is coming for dinner.

Robert says he'll buy him a plane ticket to Houston. "While you're sitting there in the snow, we're out drinking lemonade in the yard. It's eighty degrees here. The rest would do you good. We'd love to see you."

"I can afford my own plane tickets. You can't."

"That's not the point."

"No, the point is I've got a new project and I can't get away just now. But thank you."

"Are you sure you're all right?"

"Pure as a nun."

When he'd asked the doctor if he believed in transcendence, the man just frowned at him.

The new project is not entirely a fiction. He imagines a small canvas with heroic proportions of paint. Brevity at length. An impossibility on the face of it, but of course that's what makes it worth trying.

Late in the afternoon, on his way home from the medical lab, he stops by the market, starts to buy ground beef, then figures what the hell? Go for the veal. Who's around to complain of extravagance? Maybe tomorrow he'll even visit a record store – *are* there record stores, still? – and choose a Kipnis album.

On the walk outside his building the neighbor girl passes him on her shiny purple bike. She waves.

His ceiling has torn another half-inch.

He reads in the paper that Phillip, Kenneth, and Jane have jumped ship. As a group they've signed with the Herstand Gallery for an undisclosed record sum. Well. Good for them.

Long after dinner (he's saved the veal, finished the chili), he picks up his pen. Last week, six painters and four writers joined a crowd of tourists waiting to see the White House, then stepped out of line and unfurled a banner urging nuclear disarmament. The protest was coordinated with a similar one in Moscow's Red Square. The Russian demonstrators were arrested then quickly released; their American counterparts were charged with illegal entry and jailed for thirty hours. The government has threatened them with one-year prison terms. All night he drafts a letter to the President, complaining about the ham-handed treatment his colleagues have received. Yapping at the heels of federal abuse. It is a grave and fitful business, being a citizen of the world, especially in the late twentieth century.

He uncorks a bottle of wine, beats a rapid drum solo on the dirty steel pot on his stove. His abdomen kinks. He is, of course, dying. There is much to be done. He toasts the seen, the known, the heard. It is four A.M.

PAINT US A PICTURE

ANCER SLOWS PAINTER. This headline appeared in the *Houston Post* a day after Frederick Becker arrived in Texas for treatment at the M. D. Anderson Medical Center. As he read about his illness, he wondered how soon his obituary would come, and how large it would be. Would it lift him or drown him in the mud? Early in his career he'd set a rule for himself based on his first bitter experiences in New York City: never speak to journalists. Like actresses, whom he also avoided, they burn for attention, so they're always indiscreet.

In the case of the *Post* reporter, an eager wreck of a man in his late forties, Frederick made an exception. The fellow had caught him in one of the med center's many parking lots; Frederick had just finished a frank discussion with a surgeon who'd told him his chances of surviving the cancer were slim, and he felt vulnerable, beyond all rules, in need of immediate human contact.

"All my life I've wanted to be Ernest Hemingway," the reporter confided in him – a ploy to earn his trust? In the noon sun the men sat on a curb like a pair of melting lozenges. "As a result, I'm a tremendous fisherman, I have a permanent limp from a climbing accident, and I'm a recovering alcoholic. For all that, I'm still writing crap for a crappy paper."

This was a standard profile of most male journalists Frederick had encountered over the years. Once, in the early seventies, a *New York Times* reporter who'd tried to interview him confessed, "I have a basement full of stuffed marlins I've caught, all because of Papa. Still, I'm stuck writing features. Does anyone take features seriously? Do you? Be honest."

The man limped from an old boating accident. Frederick fled his misery, as he'd fled most writers since roughly 1959. On that hot afternoon in Houston, though, shaken and weak, he'd told the *Post*, "Here's the end of the story. I dribble a bit more paint, then go away."

The reporter, no Papa, wrote: "In both his art and his personal demeanor, Frederick Becker has always strived to rise above conventional norms. Disease, however, is a great leveler. The well-known smirk is now a simple grin, and the rebellious, unruly beard has shriveled into a neat white square, the like of which might adorn the chin of any distinguished lawyer."

Frederick was furious about the article, right up until the week he died.

2.

On a steaming Houston morning, a first-of-the-month Tuesday, Robert Becker opened the *Times* and counted Frederick's columns.

Three and a half, page A22. No photo.

When Motherwell died, he was granted a front page picture

plus all six columns on B9. Of course, Motherwell had established himself as a prominent critic as well as a painter. Extra duty so he'd guarantee extra coverage, the sly, lovely son of a bitch.

Late in the day, reporters from all over the country phoned Robert for a reaction to his father's death. Tersely he shared his grief, then added, to perk himself up, "I'm also a painter. In a sense, my father lives on through me."

"Right, son," said a gritty old editor at the *Kansas City Star.* "I had ambitions once too. I used to hang around Spain's brightest bodegas, hoping to soak up the aura. *Nada nada nada,* you know what I mean? Now I got a liver the size of Madrid."

All week the ghost in the nation's dailies failed to match the man Robert knew. The "brooding," "enigmatic," "reclusive," "energetic talent" the memorialists celebrated was strictly the East Coast Frederick, the late-night worrier spotted with cadmium blue, not the pale pink part-time dad who returned to Texas whenever his boy needed a birthday gift, or a graduation party or a best man at his wedding – or finally, when he himself needed the finest cancer specialists in the world.

"These doctors deserve every bit of their brilliant reputation," Frederick told Robert over dinner one evening after a day of machines at the med center. The famous gaze was fully glazed and Frederick's flesh looked tired. "Unfortunately, as with artists, it's in the nature of their work that most of the time they fail."

3.

The week Frederick died, Robert walked six miles each day from his house to Buffalo Bayou downtown. The muddy stream, running through most of the city's industrial neighborhoods, was junked with rusty old Weed-Eaters, car doors, freezers, twisted refrigerator shelves. Robert knew a shaded spot where he could be alone with the Frederick he remembered – not always pleasurably, he was startled to find. In fact, in these hours of quiet mourning, his most vivid memory turned out to be of a time, over twenty years ago, when he was certain his father would be murdered.

It started when Frederick agreed to teach a short course, in the winter of '71, at Houston's Now Arts Museum. At that point he'd been long away from Texas, in touch with Robert and his mother only on special occasions. The museum held a gala ball for what the *Post* later called "Becker's triumphant return to the city of his youth."

Robert, then fifteen, had enrolled in Frederick's course (it was held after school) but he'd used the name "Smith" on all his official forms. He didn't want his classmates to know he was the great man's son; he hoped to sit quietly, unnoticed, in the rear of the studio and learn.

For the ball, the museum rented a spacious room at the Warwick Hotel. A jazz combo, hidden by two tall ficuses in a corner by the door, played "Misty." Their every tune was "Misty." Giant reproductions of Klimt and de Kooning women lined the walls, along with papier-mâché cowboys rustling steer.

"Ah, Ruth." Frederick embraced Robert's mother as soon as she arrived. "How are you?"

"At sea," Ruth said, stepping out of his arms. "Of course, Robbie and I read in the papers you were coming, but you didn't phone or write . . . will you be wanting my guest room?"

He'd stayed there once, years ago. The lilt in Ruth's voice didn't hide the heavy ordnance in her question.

"Thank you, Ruth, no. I'm only in town for a couple of weeks. The museum's putting me up here at the Warwick."

"I see," Ruth said. "In other words, you're traveling with a woman."

Frederick frowned at her, then turned and shook Robert's hand.

All evening Ruth sat by a wall beneath a wild de Kooning siren, watching Frederick dance with one young lady after another. She'd never forgiven him for leaving her to further his career in New York. Sometimes Robert shared her resentment, but tonight he was simply glad to see his dad. He saw a tall, sharp-boned woman tug his sleeve by the ficuses. "I have a secret desire, almost a physical itch, to paint," she said breathlessly, touching his arm. "But right now I'm pursuing a life in the theatre."

"An actress." Frederick smiled. Gently, he spun her around and pushed her toward the door. She walked away, confused.

Frederick brought Ruth a glass of iced apple cider. "Care to dance, Ruthie? They've played our song all night. Maybe this time they'll get it right."

She didn't say anything. Robert was happy to see her rise and take his father's hand, but minutes later she was shoving him away. "Broadway babes!" she yelled above a shrill piano trill. "Selfish ambition!" She gripped her empty cider cup like an ice cream scoop and brought it perilously close to Frederick's right eye.

The other dancers stared. Ruth quickly recovered her calm. She told Frederick not to call her again. "I don't want to be there when some spurned little groupie finally decides to shoot you," she said. After that, the ball whirled and sparkled warmly except for a brief incident which Robert later recalled as the first flicker of danger. A young man with thick red hair and a stiff suit approached Frederick to say hello. "I've enrolled in your class, Mr. Becker. My name's Raymond. Raymond Purcell. I can't tell you how thrilled I am to meet you. You hold a very special place in my heart." His hands trembled so badly, he dropped and broke his cup. "I'm terribly sorry," he said. "I'm nervous as a mouse. I think you're America's finest painter, really I do, the colors, the scope, the sweep of your work – "

Frederick smiled and nodded, embarrassed. Raymond swept the shattered glass into his palm, but never took his eyes off the man Robert thought of, proudly, as *mine*.

Frederick opened the first class pacing the airy studio. His steps echoed beneath the high wooden ceiling. With difficulty he pocketed a round car key, mumbled something about "too many churches in Texas" and "why I left this goddamn place." He didn't seem to realize other people were in the room. His hands shook. Shaving cuts formed a little jigsaw puzzle on his neck, just below his beard. Robert smelled booze on his breath. Twenty minutes passed before Frederick settled down – before he'd even *look* at his class. Then, in the time it takes to clean a brush, he was focused, alert, all business. The lessons had begun.

He assigned each student individual projects. One woman's colors clashed; Frederick restricted her to different shades of brown. He forced another woman to slather oil on paper, to break her attachment to thin, pale lines.

"Anyone in the country can paint a beautiful picture," he announced. "We're after the not-so-beautiful that's also somehow lovely."

He told Robert to "paint the unpaintable." When Robert asked for details, Frederick answered, "You show *me*, Mr. Smith. If you want to pass this course, get to work."

Robert's talent was for portraits – faces, profiles, surfaces. He assumed his father meant for him to get *inside* the people he painted, to expose the edges and hues of their angers and loves.

In the sunny studio, Raymond Purcell's spongy red hair was afire. His body bobbed with excitement whenever Frederick spoke, as if buffeted by the sound of his voice. Raymond didn't receive an assignment; Frederick said he had a remarkable style, and should just keep painting what he wanted. Robert felt jealous, especially as he'd landed the hardest task of all. Did this mean he had the most to learn?

He was shocked to see the actress in class, the woman Frederick had pushed from the room the night of the ball. "It turns out, she's serious about learning," Frederick told Robert when the first meeting was over. They were driving in a rented Dodge, on their way to the Warwick. "In my experience, actresses are the least serious people in the world. Jill is a pleasant surprise."

In his room, Frederick fixed himself a Scotch and soda. Robert grabbed a Milky Way bar and a Coke from the portable refrigerator by the bed. When he was nine or ten, his father scolded him for eating too much candy, for being overweight. Robert was thin now, but he held the candy bar out of sight between his knees, still anticipating disapproval.

"It was a shaky start," Frederick admitted. "It's been years since I've spoken to a group. I was nervous. Needed a little something to steel myself. Did I embarrass you?"

"You did fine."

Frederick opened the closet door. "See?" he said. "No harem. No hidden mistresses. Just lonely old me."

Through the window Robert watched the looping grids of Houston's streets.

"How *is* your mother?" Frederick asked. "Since she won't speak to me, you'll have to be my spy."

"She's okay. She says you left her high and dry, but I think she's learned to live without you all right."

"And you?"

Robert shrugged. "I guess you knew what you needed."

"The thing is, when two people live together as long as we did, one's voice becomes background noise to the other, like an all-day radio," Frederick said. "Soon, they're only half listening to each other. 'What, what?' – the single most common utterance in marriage. I couldn't stand a lifetime of 'what,' Robbie. It's as simple as that."

He poured himself another Scotch. Below and all around, Houston's lights throbbed like clusters of fireflies swimming out of the dark. "On the other hand, comfort's harder to find than you think. I'm an old man now." He was forty in '71. "These days I'll see an attractive woman on the street and try to catch her attention, but she glides right by. It's shameless, the way the young only want the young, like some abominable herding instinct. What about the rest of us?" He sipped his drink. "You definitely know when you're out of the hunt. It's not a choice you make."

Robert recalled all the young women eager to dance with his father at the ball, and the actress, Jill Ryne, placing her hand on his arm, but he didn't say anything. Frederick seemed convinced of being, as he put it, a "sexual cast-off." The more he drank, the more depressed he became. Robert wanted to ask his dad's opinion of his work, but the Old Master was clearly stuck in his sadness.

In the next few days Robert got to know his classmates. They'd go for sandwiches, share what they'd learned. They all agreed that Mr. Becker was a magnificent teacher, magnetic and inspiring (if a little offbeat). They wanted to ask him to join them some night, but were too intimidated to approach him personally. Robert could've asked, but he was enjoying meeting new friends; he knew if Frederick came along he'd dominate every conversation. At the end of each class he watched his father frown and slink away to the parking lot alone, to go drink in his room. Robert had seen the roses Frederick sent Ruth after the ball. She'd tossed them out with the coffee grounds. "All drunks are sentimental," she said. Still, it was hard to believe that a man as brilliant as his dad could remain unhappy for long.

Raymond Purcell was the only member of the class who didn't socialize with the others. He always looked spent when the sessions were through, limp in his chair, as though he'd been beaten instead of steadily encouraged.

As Frederick said, Jill Ryne was the nicest surprise in the group. "I used to be a painter's model," she told Robert. "One morning I realized the painter was having more fun than I was, playing with his colors while I sat there freezing my ass off in that big, drafty room." She always wore a black ribbon around her neck to highlight her bone-white skin, the most erotic sight Robert had ever seen. She joked about being old – at twenty-five, and with a birthday just around the bend, she was the senior member of the class. Robert felt giddy whenever she laughed or looked at him and smiled. She was kind to everyone, but seemed especially warm with him. One night after dinner with their pals she dropped him off at Ruth's house. When he opened the car door she kissed his cheek, just a friendly peck, but he was so excited he couldn't find the curb, and slipped on the soft front lawn.

4.

Buffalo Bayou winds around cotton warehouses, rice mills, freeway overpasses, clumps of blooming dogwood. Herons rise from thin brown reeds along its banks, possums skitter over plastic garbage bags, Pepsi, Coors, and tuna fish cans. Flies circle an old, abandoned shoe, buzzing like cracked cellos.

Robert sits and stares into the water. Brown and orange eddies – mud and rust – stir wild rose petals in pools around warped coffee tables, Volkswagen fenders, jackets and knives, tires and old bicycle pumps. People dump this stuff for convenience or fun; the stream is a living collage of color and shape.

Frederick, dredged from memory, drifts near the bottom by a hot water heater, wearing a striped wool shirt and khaki-colored pants. He claws his way toward the surface, past the city's cast-offs, the auto parts and toaster plugs. Twigs and silt tangle in the once-thick beard, the firm, ironic smile is now an O of fear.

A black four-door Chevy pulls swiftly off the freeway, stops, raising dust. Robert slaps mosquitoes from his wrists. Two young men drag a busted vacuum cleaner from the Chevy's trunk and heave it into the bayou, at the spot where Robert imagined his father. The men grunt and spit. When they're gone, Robert stands and watches the ripples. Frederick, cut and bleeding, paddles back into his head. He lifts his arms to the sky. *Robbie,* he mouths. *Lend me a hand. Please, Robbie. Save me.* Bubbles erupt from his throat. O. O.

5.

One day, in the second week of class, Jill leaned past Robert to smooth a charcoal line on her sketch pad, and he caught a shot of her breasts beneath her smock. She saw him look, smiled. He turned away, embarrassed, but felt he'd received a brief, sweet blessing.

"He assigned me set designs, backdrops for plays," she said. "Sunsets, stars."

She drew perfectly lovely clouds, Robert thought, but how hard is a cloud? She'd gotten off lightly. Nothing like painting the unpaintable. Frustrated with his own assignment, he spent studio time sketching Jill's neck. Her birthday was two days away. "An early gift," he said, handing her the drawings. She blushed. "You're a sweet boy," she told him, and kissed his cheek.

Frederick asked Robert to go help Raymond. Robert caught a tang of Scotch in the air, beneath the drifting smells of chalk dust and oils, radiator heat and fresh breezes from the windows. "I can show you a better sky," Frederick promised Jill, pulling up a stool. She beamed.

Under his smock, Raymond had on the same stiff suit he'd worn at the ball, and to every class so far. His hands twitched with nervous energy, rattling the legs of his easel. "I want to kill him," he whispered. "Wring his goddamn neck. I'm letting him down, letting him down . . ."

Robert was astonished by the work: flat, nearly colorless eggs curled across solid black backgrounds. Raymond had gouged each canvas with a palette knife, to interrupt the surface. Robert saw no balance here. *This* was a remarkable style?

Raymond laughed when Robert described his own project. "That's not an assignment, it's a chisel in the heart, man." His red hair bounced above his ears.

A tight, cold pain seized Robert's stomach and balls. He rose, mumbling "water" and "excuse me." Raymond returned to his canvases, whispering, "Twist his silly neck till his Adam's apple pops to the floor."

———

That evening Robert heated himself a chicken pot pie, scarfed it down, and told his mother he was going to catch a bus to the Warwick. Ruth had meant to serve stew. She stood in a bright orange apron, holding a spoon, watching Robert finish his pie. "If you're looking for his approval, Robbie, you might as well know he'll never give it. That's him, not you. God forbid he should ever admit he cares for anyone."

Robert set his plate in the sink.

Softly, Ruth touched his shoulder, his back. "I should've thought twice about letting you take this class."

"He's a good teacher."

"Good to all the young women, I'll bet. He's never learned to act his age."

Her bitterness was like an extra roll of insulation in the ceiling, trapping heat. Robert snatched a sweater from his closet and ran from the house.

Late-season fireflies swirled above Buffalo Bayou; Houston's winter was typically mild. The bus chugged past the stream, under live oaks and willows, streetlights haloed in mist. Robert drew his father's face in the moisture on the glass. A stern, disenchanted stare.

The Warwick looked like a party cake, bright yellow windows in curves of smooth white stone. The moment he stepped off the elevator near Frederick's room, Robert saw Raymond Purcell pacing by a failed ficus in a corner of the hallway. His suit was wrinkled and dirty. He held a large portfolio case. "Smith!" he said, moving quickly as a bee, grabbing Robert's arm. "What are you doing here?" His breath smelled of coffee and pickles.

"I'm . . . I have an appointment," Robert said.

"You do?"

"Yes."

"You do? He gives appointments?"

"What about you?"

A large, erratic vein pulsed in Raymond's forehead. "I see his disappointment, you know . . . I want to *strangle* him sometimes." He shook his fist at Frederick's door. "I wish he'd . . . appointments? Jesus Christ, he gives *appointments?* Why didn't he tell me?" He snapped and unsnapped his case, shook his head, then strode past Robert toward the stairway. "Oh God, he hates me. I know it. America's finest painter, my one chance, and he . . . oh my God, oh God I want to kill him. Tell him, Smith. Tell him I want to see him." He disappeared down the stairwell.

When Frederick answered Robert's knock he was carrying the phone. "Yes, Ruth, that's all I want too." He motioned Robert into the room. Robert veered toward the tiny icebox for chocolate and a Coke. His hands trembled from the force of Raymond's outburst.

"Ruth, Ruthie please, don't hang up," Frederick said. "I'm *trying* to be friends." He lowered his voice, glanced at his boy. "I never stopped loving him, you know that. And you, Ruth. Dear Ruth. It hurts that you won't even see me." A minute later he set the receiver in its cradle. "Well." He rubbed his face.

He'd cut himself shaving again; a drop of blood dyed the tip of his collar. "She's worried about you."

Robert gobbled the last of a Snickers. He remembered eating greedily as a child so his father wouldn't catch him, swallowing so rapidly the candy had no taste. Always, whenever his father entered a room, Robert's belly felt leaden but empty.

"She asked me when you got here to – oh hell. Do I treat you all right, Robbie? Do you ever doubt how important you are to me?"

"No." Robert shoved the Snickers wrapper deep into a pocket of his jeans. "It's just that sometimes I wonder what you honestly – "

"Good," Frederick said, brightening. "Good. I tried to tell her. Your mother's just a worrywart." He walked, quick and suddenly sure, across the room. He wouldn't look at Robert. "Now, what do you say I fix myself a drink, then we go for a ride, eh? I've only got a few days left here in the old hometown. I'd like to see some sights." He opened a bottle of Dewar's.

"Dad." Robert rarely used the word. It felt like day-old gum in his mouth.

"Yes?"

"I guess Raymond Purcell's a pretty good painter, huh?"

Frederick shrugged, busy with the ice.

Robert didn't know what he wanted to say, exactly. He blurted, too loudly, "I worry about him."

"Why's that?"

"I don't know. Doesn't he seem . . . a little dangerous to you?"

"How?"

"I'm not sure, but maybe you'd better be careful. I think he wants to hurt you."

Frederick raised a pointed eyebrow.

"I know it sounds crazy, but he's worked himself up so much trying to please you, and he thinks . . . he thinks you're not happy with his progress, like you're punishing him and he can't understand why." In the rush of his words, Robert felt the beginnings of tears. He was so surprised by this, he sat on the bed to keep from losing his balance. He caught his breath. "He just wants to know."

Frederick looked at him, only for a moment, then smiled. "So he's angry with me?"

Robert shook his head. "Not – " He blinked a few times. "I don't know. He's making threats."

Frederick sniffed his booze. "You don't suppose this is poisoned, do you? Quick, call the *Post*. If I die before they arrive, it's up to you to see they get my story straight. I want a glowing obit, photo and all."

Robert brushed his nose with the back of his hand. Frederick patted his arm. "Okay. Thanks for the warning, Robbie. I appreciate it."

They took the rented Dodge into the cool night air, past shopping malls, construction cranes, chapels. "I can't get over how religious Texas is," Frederick said. "I'd forgotten, completely. Look at the steeples! And down in the cellars, Methodists, Lutherans, Catholics, Baptists stirring vats of potato salad. Hundreds of believers mixing the vile yellow stuff to sling at unrepentant sinners. We'd best arm ourselves, Robbie. They're bound to come after us."

Blow after blow of his usual wit – as if his sincerity in the room had been a joke. I might as well stay Mr. Smith, Robert thought. He felt no bonds with the man here beside him or the mighty Becker name.

"When I was your age, Robbie, this very spot was an occasion of sin for me." Frederick pulled off the highway, to a dark gravel patch on the banks of Buffalo Bayou. "One night I stole my father's Buick and a bottle of sour mash and went for a joyride. It ended right here. There wasn't a freeway then, just a dirt road by the stream. I back-ended another happy drunk. Ruined the front fender. My father never forgave me."

He got out and headed for the bayou. Robert followed. Frederick sat beneath a large live oak and began to remove his shoes and socks. "The other fellow and I lay here for an hour or so, laughing about the accident, sharing our whiskey. It was a cool night like tonight but we barely felt it, dipped our feet in the shallows – ah! – and watched the moon, big and yellow, sail above the trees."

Robert listened to his father splash the water, scanned the tires and busted chairs that broke the surface of the stream. He found the candy bar wrapper in his pocket and quietly dropped it on the ground.

"Join me?" Frederick said

Robert shook his head.

"You're an awfully sober young man, you know that? Do you smoke or drink, Robbie?"

"No."

"That's good, I suppose. Healthy." He wiggled his toes. "Don't you ever get tired of being good?"

Always riding me, Robert thought. How do I get *inside* this man, past all the layers of irony?

Frederick sighed and stretched his arms. "This is a nice, shady place in the daytime. Your mother and I used to come here."

"Really?" Robert sat. "She won't let you make up with her?"

"No, no. Too *many* sins." Frederick said nothing for a minute. Frogs chirped in the reeds. When he did speak, he almost whispered. "In those days, when your mom and I were courting, this whole area was quite romantic. Bluebonnets. Tall grass. It's tragic, what people have done to it. What's that sticking out of the mud over there?"

"Looks like an air-conditioner," Robert said.

Frederick shook his head. "Ruthie and I watched sunsets here, a million years ago. Silly kids. Well." He reached for his socks. "Best to let it all go."

Touched by his father's nostalgia, Robert searched the weeds for his candy wrapper. "The city should clean this place," he said, attempting to imagine a shining blue bayou, his father and mother holding hands beneath swelling Gulf Coast clouds.

"A guy like Rauschenberg would know what to do with this stuff. He'd haul it all out and make something with it. If we knew how to look, Robbie, we'd see endless possibilities in this wonderful, wretched stream. I envy sculptors. They can redeem the most useless junk." Frederick laughed and clapped Robert's back. "Sin and redemption, eh?" He frowned. "Why are you so quiet?"

Robert shook his head.

"Raymond?"

"No."

"Is it your mother?"

"Not really."

Frederick stood and stroked his beard. "I see. You came over tonight to talk about your work, didn't you?"

Robert lost his mental portrait of his fresh young parents. "Yes."

"You feel the assignment's too hard?"

"I don't know what I feel. Maybe." He followed his father back to the car.

"None of us ever learn enough about what we're doing, Robbie." Frederick threw his boots onto the slick back seat. "Not even Picasso or Matisse. But don't worry." He turned the key. The engine coughed. "I know how the story ends."

It was after eleven when Frederick dropped him off at Ruth's house. Robert invited him in but Frederick said no. As he pulled away he waved and gave a weak smile. Ruth was still up, stirring stew. She'd already made three pots, with ham and carrots and peas. "It's late. I was starting to worry," she said. When Robert told her where they'd gone, she cursed Frederick for dragging him out in the cold. Then she smiled, remembering the spot. "It *was* a special place."

"It's trashed now," Robert told her. "What made it so special?"

"Oh, I don't know if it's the setting so much." She tapped her wooden spoon on the stove. "We were young and happy . . . a little careless. I think you were conceived there."

"Mom!"

She blushed. "Well, it was nice and lush and private. No freeway."

"Dad told me." He grinned. "So you liked him in those days?"

"Oh yes."

Robert tasted the stew. "And now?"

"Don't be taken in by his charms, Robbie. He shook Texas off his boots and never looked back, once he left."

"That's not true. He's flown back plenty of times."

"He has a whole other life in New York, believe me."

"Like what?"

"Like, he married an actress soon's he got to Manhattan. That's what. Some Broadway queen."

Robert burned his lips on the clear, steaming broth. "You're kidding. But you were still married to him."

Ruth shook her head. "We'd filed our divorce papers, just barely."

"Who was she?" The peppery ham made him cough. "What was she like?"

"No idea. The marriage only lasted six months or so. I never knew what happened. All I heard was she left." She glanced at her boy, testing the effect of her words. "I guess your father got his heart broken – his drinking got worse – but I didn't want to hear it, and he won't talk about it now." She washed her hands. "He always *was* a sucker for aggressive women. Don't know why he hooked up with me."

Robert stared at the worry lines on her cheeks and chin. She dried her fingers, straightened her hair. "Anyway," she said. "It's over and done. Time for bed." He squeezed her hand. For a moment in the flat kitchen light she looked, despite her worn face, like a sad little girl, pale as dough, waiting to be taken, shaped, gracefully held. She turned out all the lights and hugged him goodnight.

6.

He can't imagine his father's second wife without also smelling his mother's mushrooms, carrots, potatoes simmering on her stove. This afternoon, as he walks along the stream, humming some half-remembered tune, he realizes Frederick's New York years are an empty space to him, an unmarked corner of a canvas. Robert sees his father walking in the city, working there with ease, unburdened by the doubts that paralyze *him* in his studio at home until he often wonders if he can go on.

He kicks a rusty crankshaft. Mud-sprinkles scatter tiny blue-flies through the air, stir the bayou's oily brown waves. Down below, his father floats. O. O. *Robbie. Save me. Lend me a hand.*

All day, people have tossed broken steam irons, croquet mallets, skillets, ax blades chipped and bent into the swirling silt. Each time a man or woman hurls an object into the water, Robert remembers a recent newspaper phrase: "Becker was simply in the right spot at the right historical moment"; "The late Frederick Becker is little more than a footnote to contemporary American painting"; "If Pollock was genuinely witty, then Becker is merely amusing."

Other obituaries have lavishly praised Frederick's work, but the barbs are blunt steel to Robert. Cold and unforgiving, precisely aimed, like steam irons and skillets. He watches mosquitoes skim the water's thickness. Frederick drifts in tattered algae. *Robbie, don't let them bury me. It's up to you to see they get my story straight.* The ax blade shoots past his ear. A mallet slams his thin, bluing chest.

Robert shuts his mind to his father's cries. Memories are starting to rise that he knows are no good, old furies about to riddle the day. He paces the banks of the bayou, tries to concentrate on birdsong, water splash, sunlight. The melodies that have haunted him all morning. But the bubbles erupt.

7.

It was the night of Jill's birthday. Robert and his classmates, all except Raymond, had gathered early at the sandwich shop to arrange a surprise. Robert brought party hats and bright red balloons. The waiters agreed to sing "Happy Birthday" as loudly and embarrassingly as possible when she walked in the door, but at 8:30 she still hadn't shown, and by nine everyone was restless. "Wasn't she planning to come?" someone asked. "Did anyone see her after class?"

"Yeah. She was talking to Mr. Becker."

"Where?"

"In the parking lot, outside the studio."

The door slid open, ringing a dwarf silver bell attached to the frame. Cool air brushed the tables and chairs. A flicker of red. A goofy grin. "Hi," Raymond said. "I hoped you'd all still be here." The class stared. He laughed – almost a bray. "Have you already eaten?"

A brief, edgy silence. Then the students rose to leave, saying it was late. Blushing, Raymond stared at the floor. "I'm sorry," he said. "Sorry. I know I haven't been very friendly. I just hoped to accomplish something while we had him in our midst, that's all. I didn't mean to snub any of you. Honest." His loafers creaked.

No one moved or knew what to say. A waiter who'd heard the bell emerged from the kitchen with a square of ginger cake. He began to sing the birthday song, then caught his mistake.

The place was so quiet, Robert heard pipes in the walls knocking with steam, water tapping in a sink. "Mr. Know-It-All," one of his classmates said.

"Mr. *Style,*" said another.

Raymond shivered. Robert touched his sleeve. "Can you drop me somewhere?" he asked.

"Sure," Raymond said. Relieved, people reached for their coats then quickly, silently left.

Raymond led Robert to his car, an old Ford Mustang. It smelled of linseed oil. Crammed into the back, sketch pads, charcoals. Stiff, used brushes, some the size of housepainter's tools. His foot twitched on the accelerator; the car hiccuped and jerked.

Robert's belly ached with Jill's absence. He'd hoped to get her alone later, maybe guide her to the bayou, hold her hand in the dark, but she had her eye on someone else.

He asked Raymond to take him to the studio; from there, he'd walk the few blocks to the Warwick.

Maybe he was wrong.

"I'm glad it's nearly over," Raymond said. A light mist peppered the streets. He switched on his wipers. "The class, I mean. I'm exhausted."

"Me too," Robert said.

"Who needs him, anyway? He can't appreciate what I do. So what? It's not like he's God." The Mustang lurched through a dull yellow light. "I mean, you cut him and he bleeds like anyone else, right?"

Robert's skin tightened and his throat went dry. Raymond gripped the wheel like a strangler. He was scowling, no longer the pathetic figure Robert had seen in the sandwich shop. He seemed, as he always did in class, malevolent, deceitful; his red hair a stain against decency and reason. Somehow, his presence made the streets chaotic and mean. The city's old grid pattern clashed with the new, north/south blocking east and west. In parks and at bus stops, people clung to each other in the rapidly cooling air, men and women, women and kids, ragged Pietàs.

"I've always trusted myself," Raymond said, slowing for another light. The mist was twice as dense as it was a moment ago. "Never needed anyone's approval, so why start now?" His right foot stopped twitching. He reached into his coat pocket for something apparently heavy (the weapon he might've clocked Frederick with, Robert thought); his shoulders tensed. He sidled close with a grin.

Robert didn't wait to see what happened next. "Thanks," he said, unlocking his door. "This is good." He stumbled onto the pavement.

"Hey!" Raymond called. "Are you crazy? Watch out!"

Robert ran down the street through folds of bleak gray air. Car horns barked. A pair of headlights swung in an arc to his right, then whirled out of sight. "Asshole!" someone yelled. He sprinted against the evening's stinging wet until his whole chest burned and he saw the yellow windows of the Warwick. The doorman, dressed in red, tipped his tricorn hat but Robert hustled past him, grunting. His muddy shoes soiled the thick blue carpet.

He bounded up the stairs to Frederick's floor, half-searching for clues to Raymond's foul deed, but there were no abandoned knives. No gory gloves.

In front of his father's door he found an awful mess. He dropped, gasping, to his knees.

Two tall-stemmed glasses on a thin silver tray. Crumbs. A pale pink candle, never lit.

He groaned and got to his feet. Just go home, he thought. Leave it alone. He sidestepped the ficus and pounded on the door.

At first, no sounds came from the room. Then Frederick's voice, muffled, "Go away."

"It's me." Robert hit the door again. "It's Mr. Smith. I've come for my grade."

"Robbie?"

"I want to talk to you."

"Just a minute."

Behind the door, glass broke. Robert swayed. His lungs still ached from his run. Frederick stepped out bleeding.

"My God," Robert said. "What – ?"

"Sliced my hand on the Dewar's," Frederick said. He wore a towel around his waist. He was musky and sweetly perfumed, a swarming, cloying smell, all at once. "Damned annoying. Waste of good Scotch." In his wounded palm he clutched a roiling cloud of toilet paper. Blood smeared his chest. "What's so urgent? What are you doing here?"

Robert leaned against the wall. He felt foolish and weak. "Dad?"

"Robbie, what is it?"

"I need to know something."

"What?"

"Have you seen Jill Ryne?"

Frederick blinked as if sprayed with a hose. He made a fist of his bloody hand. "Of course not. Why?"

Robert kicked the tray, crushing one of the champagne glasses. Frederick jumped. "I have to know the truth. Have you *seen* her?"

"All right, yes, yes," Frederick answered. "She's here with me, okay? She's fine. Nothing to worry about."

Robert went again to his knees, this time with a harder pain to find, but no less solid than the bite in his lungs.

"Robbie – "

"You son of a bitch." He reached up and slapped his dad.

The stiff beard raked his fingers like the bristles of a camel's-hair brush. Frederick was sleepy and drunk. He fell against the door, into the room. A shadow rustled by the bed. Robert felt Jill's presence, vital and near. He remembered the golden shade of the tops of her breasts, her friendly smile, and kicked the tray again. "Robbie, for God's sake, what's gotten into you?" Frederick tried to sit up.

"Mom was right about you all along!"

"Your mother? What about her? Robbie, help me up."

"You and your not-so-beautiful bull and your *actresses!*" Robert yelled.

Frederick grabbed the doorknob, raised himself nearly to his feet. "Robbie. Wait here. Let me get dressed, then we'll go for a drink. Let's talk, okay? Robbie? Please?"

8.

[Becker sniffs his fingers. "Every woman I've ever touched," he says. "Every painting I've ever made. Amazing how they linger in the skin." Pause.]

Reporter: My sources here at the med center – friends, really – tell me you're suffering from cancer.

Becker: Bloody mort men.

Reporter: Sir?

Becker: Death-beat. Obits. The *Post* sent you to put me in the ground.

Reporter: No.

Becker: What's your name, Papa?

Reporter: Chuck.

Becker: Chuck, what's a good mort man earn these days?

Reporter: I wouldn't know.

Becker: Life's sweeter as there's less and less time. You can print that.

Reporter: If you were to sum up your career –

Becker: I'm in no particular hurry, thanks.

Reporter: It would help our readers if, in the article, I could pin you to certain historical –

Becker: History's already pinned me, Chuck. I don't need any pinning from you.

[Pause. Becker sniffs his fingers again.]

Reporter: Okay, then, can you tell me what you feel is your finest achievement?

Becker: The fact that I've accumulated only twenty years of regrets, rather than thirty or forty.

Reporter: Regrets about what?

Becker: Art and family. What else is there?

9.

Before the final class, Jill pulled Robert aside in a far, cobwebby corner of the studio to assure him she was the same person she always was. "I hope we can still be pals," she said.

Robert didn't understand. "You slept with him," he whispered. "How can you say you haven't changed?"

"Who'd you think I was?" She looked nervous and tired. "Robbie – "

"I thought you liked me." He knew he sounded childish, and he hated himself.

"I do, but I'm so much older – "

Robert shook his head then turned away.

"And who are you," Jill said, "to go banging on people's doors in the middle of the night and to stand here like Jesus Christ, telling me my business . . . you have no right to judge me, Robert Becker!"

His own name startled him.

"That's right, your father told me. Who's the *real* actor here? If you've got a problem, it's between the two of you." She marched across the studio to her supply table; the sound of her steps bounced off the sheer, dusty walls. She found Robert's drawings of her and shoved them at his chest. "Take these," she said. "We'll have to clear out all our stuff after class."

Remarkably, Frederick was fit and alert, no longer the bleeding drunk of the evening before, but king of his domain once more, witty, quick, and sure. He glanced at Robert once, but otherwise conducted himself with detachment and élan. "Fly, fly away," he told the class. "And good luck."

At the break, Raymond offered Robert his hand. "I wish you well with your work," he said. "I don't know where you were off to in such a hurry last night, but I meant to give you this." He reached into his pocket for a purple cloth sack of milk chocolates. He'd bought everyone in the class a tiny pouch of sweets. Later, Robert learned he'd given Frederick a cassette recording of Beethoven's final string trios, Opus Three, E-Flat: Finale; Opus Eight, D-Major: Pollaca; and Opus Nine, Number One, G-Major, along with a note:

> Something for you. I edited Opus Numbers Three and Eight to keep the performance to ninety minutes, but feel justified because the Maestro didn't hit his stride in this genre until Opus Nine anyway. May you find the same confidence and energy in them that I have.
>
> Thank you for your time these last two weeks. I've learned from you that art is a by-product of the artist's struggle to understand his pain, and that both the struggle and the pain are meaningless.
>
> Mr. Becker, pick up your brush.
> Show us why we matter.
> Show us how to be.
> Paint us a picture.

By session's end, Raymond was twitching uncontrollably – nervousness? loneliness? uncertainty? He fumbled his palette, smearing black in the deep wrinkles of his dropcloth. Despite his dark disappointments, he watched Frederick with what Robert recognized as honest, eager love.

He never posed any danger, Robert thought. *I'm* the one who wants to kill the old man.

"I said goodbye to your mother. This morning, on the phone," Frederick told Robert when the others had left.

"I know."

"You didn't mention – ?"

"Last night? No." He capped a can of turpentine, packed his paints.

Frederick nodded. "Still, she seems to think it's best if I stay away from Texas for a while."

"Too many churches," Robert said. "And not enough Broadway, I suppose."

Frederick smiled. "I'm a double-minded man, Robbie, always torn – like this music." He tapped Raymond's tape. "I know this. Sprightly and sad. It's a good choice for me." Years later, as he was dying in the hospital, he requested the string trios. Robert brought a portable tape player to his room. "Listen. Do you hear how harshly the melody fights itself?" Frederick said. "Like a madman shaking his fist at a world he knows he loves too much."

That day in the studio he opened his arms. "What can I say?" he told Robert. "Usually I resist because I've learned how much attention a woman like Jill demands – more than one man can give – but they're so inherently dramatic. Spicy. Beats back the humdrum, temporarily."

Robert wiped his hands on a rag. "Are you going to see her before you leave?"

"Your mother?"

"No."

"Oh. Yes. She's adept at pretending, Robbie. Gives me the illusion I'm desired. Again, temporarily." The big, empty room was stuffy and hot. It smelled like a freshly painted gymnasium. Frederick blotted his forehead with the back of his cotton sleeve. "Anyway, congratulations. You did good work in the course."

"I didn't finish my assignment."

"No," Frederick said. "And you never will. Consider that a blessing. You have an aesthetic problem, and the talent, to engage your imagination for the rest of your life. That's more than most people have. More than that poor wretch, Raymond. Or Jill." He stepped forward; after a moment's hesitation he squeezed Robert's shoulder, kissed his cheek. "And that's the end of the story."

Robert watched him walk to the door. "One more thing,"

Frederick said, turning, scratching his ear. "You might have a tendency, from now on, to mistrust women. That's not the lesson." He smoothed his wide, imposing beard. "The lesson is, don't trust fathers."

10.

Robbie, don't leave me here.
Go away, he whispers to himself. Time to forget.
I'm drifting off . . .
"So what?" he shouts. Muscles knot his neck. He fires an old soup can into the stream – Campbell's chicken with rice, Andy Warhol's brand. It strikes Frederick's head right at the hairline. He sinks in lemon-colored foam, among sewing machines, dentist's drills, axles, wheels, ceramic brown ashtrays, picture frames, photo books – faces embedded, like flashbacks in a story, in the unforgiving movement of the present – corkscrews and can openers, steam boilers, petticoats . . .
Endless possibilities.
"Stay there!" Robert yells.
A grackle lifts above the trees. Clouds huddle like big frozen birds wrapped in white plastic in a butcher's bin.
His beginnings are lost in careless waste. He snatches from the shallows a copper pocket watch. When he opens the scratched glass face, water pours out. "Drink me," he remembers, a line from *Alice in Wonderland.* Ruth read him that story once, when he cried all night for his dad.
He plucks out a hubcap, a carpenter's file, an old apple crate, piles them together on the bank. He doesn't know if he's making a futile attempt to clean the place or if he's building a ragged monument to his origin.
He watches another grackle float above the water toward a steel-and-glass steeple miles away. The night he sat here with Frederick this particular chapel was hidden in the dark. Or maybe it hadn't been built yet. "Sin and redemption," he mutters.
A blessing, Frederick says.

Standing here in the muck and swell of his conception, he hears Beethoven's melodies rise and fall. *One more thing*, the music says, using Frederick's voice. He pictures his father in the studio, that beautiful, terrible winter of '71. *I didn't just give you the hardest assignment in the class, Robbie. It was the* only *assignment.*

Cars rattle by on the freeway, shaking the concrete pylons. In the water, Frederick's wedged against an old chest of drawers.

You were the only one who had a chance of going on, who still has that chance. Go on.

My life is full, Robert thinks.

Your life is full. Go on.

He plants his feet firmly on the mud-and-gravel bank. Cello melodies soar in his mind. He reaches down, sighs, and pulls his father from the bayou.

Almost Barcelona

At about the time his father's cancer burst uncontrollably open in colon, brain and throat, his own health began to fail. Nothing life-threatening: restlessness – a sort of itching in the skin – lack of appetite, shifting bowels. "Sick with worry," said Sarah. "Too much stress – Robbie, it's hardly coincidence."

All winter she'd waited for Robert's worries to break. In late January he'd brought his father home to Texas from the rent-controlled apartment in Manhattan. He'd arranged for round-the-clock care at the med center, and he'd temporarily suspended his own projects. His work wasn't moving much anyway – one small showing in a local gallery where, predictably, he was promoted as the son of the famous Abstract Expressionist, Frederick Becker.

Sarah, bless her, had been a tender anchor. She insisted that Robert was painting masterfully despite the slow market for his work; she patiently accepted the burden of Frederick's sickness into her life. He'd been ebbing for two years, but the final dying – the last fatal push – occurred over a six-week period.

In his dad's last days, Robert recalled how his first-grade school reports arrived in the mail every six weeks – a time-frame, filled with swift judgment, that always terrified him. "Well now, Robbie, did you finally catch fire this term?" he remembered his hard father saying.

For six weeks as Frederick shrank and Robert sat by (like a cook, he sometimes thought, watching a heavy stock boil down on a stove) Sarah paid the bills, cleaned the house – as efficiently as a Grand Prix mechanic she kept the details of Robert's life running smoothly while he said his slow goodbye.

One afternoon in the hospital, Frederick pulled Robert's face to his own. He was pale as a dime on the starchy pillow. The room smelled of mercurochrome. "I'm sorry you had to bear all this alone," Frederick whispered. The cancer had acted on his voice like a steel blade on an apple. Robert said, "Shhh" – but his father was right. His mother had died in '82; what few relatives he knew about were as vague to him as the figures Frederick sometimes buried beneath the thick red and black surfaces of his canvases.

(His father used to laugh at the "young guns" – the postwar critics – who asked in the pages of *ARTnews*, "Do these ghostly human shapes mean that Becker is abandoning pure abstraction?" In '72 – several blown-apart art movements later – Frederick did a *60 Minutes* interview in which he quipped, "Throughout my career I abandoned anything that even *smacked* of purity." This statement was taken by a new generation of critics as his credo. As perhaps it was.)

Despite his acclaim, the Becker family had always acted embarrassed by one another. Years ago they'd scattered to various poor jobs, various hills and valleys around the country.

Frederick's oldest sister, Fay, was the only relative Robert remembered with any certainty. He recalled her saying one afternoon (to whom was she speaking? where did the conversation take place?), "Modern art. It's all about sex, that's what it is. His paintings may not *look* like anything, but I know what the bastard's thinking."

For some reason, Robert's dad was the blackest sheep in a dark-wool family. Too "bohemian" perhaps, too much the "libertine" – words Robert imagined Fay using. Now that he had followed Frederick's cadmium blue trail into the House of Art, Robert was a bad lamb too.

Sarah volunteered to contact the funeral director and a lawyer. In the days immediately after Frederick's death Robert simply stopped. He felt, when he was conscious of feeling at all, that he'd stepped into a late Rothko and was wrapped in a dry black mist that reeked of turpentine and linseed oil.

———

Most of the last thirty years Frederick had lived in the West Village but Houston always had a strong, almost erotic, grip on the old bird. Wherever he traveled – Paris, San Francisco, Barcelona – wherever he was fêted for his work, he spoke fondly of Houston's trees, the wet, leafy arms of its wraparound willows. He loved too the beautiful brown skin of friendly young Chicanas in the barrios and mesquite-scented, lime-soaked fajitas. All his life he wore Tony Lama boots – a western affectation he never lost in the East.

Initially, then, Robert decided to bury Frederick in Texas next to his first wife, Robert's mother, under a sweeping live oak tree on a hill overlooking the Gulf of Mexico. At night a lighthouse beam cut through thick orange oil-refinery steam gathering in boxlike clouds over the Gulf; foghorns called in brief, sad bursts out at sea.

Less than twenty-four hours before the memorial service, however, Robert changed his mind. He reheard in memory, "When I'm gone, set me to the torch and blow away my goddamn ashes, will you?"

"Are you sure?" he asked his father.

"Absolutely."

This turned out to be the first of several dialogues Robert continued to have with him.

Frederick went on (words Robert *didn't* remember, though they had his father's stamp): "Collage. Random collision. I've devoted my whole life to them and I don't see why death should stop me. So go ahead and toss my leftovers into the stratosphere. Maybe a pinch of my old ass'll land in a lilac bush, a sniff in a pig's snout, an ounce or two in an empty bucket. Who knows – I may drift through a bus window somewhere and settle on the lap of a lusty woman off to make a killing in the market, eh? Viva collage!"

———

Sometimes at night now Robert and Sarah made slow, simple love together. More often they'd talk. Sarah told him she'd be patient until his grief let go, but he knew she was edgy and tired of the distance he'd shown since Frederick's death – giant *nothings* (both the distance and the death) that seemed to be growing.

———

This is how it started each night: he'd slide into bed, kiss Sarah's forehead and cheeks, then stare for several minutes at a screened window opening onto his yard and the little tin shed he'd converted into a studio out back. He imagined the blank or half-finished canvases in the cradles of their easels, the oily rags, the spattered palettes he'd left on his studio table.

Incomplete sketches: Sarah, his mother.

Then he'd recall, from fifteen or sixteen years ago, visits to his father's studio in New York. The place was crammed with line drawings after Paul Klee ("One bone alone achieves nothing," Klee wrote). There weren't any studies of people, no familiar faces – just deep gray strokes and sheets of cascading color on the stark white walls. Red, green, purple, and black swayed from the ceiling on unseen hooks and wires. Robert remembered seeing, against a wire-mesh window, the famous series of cadmium blue sponge-mop streaks entitled *Elegy*.

Each night now he stared, with burning eyes, at the memories of blue in his head. Lake, sea, iris blue. Eventually, the jumpy hues merged and became a sky unfolding like a blanket against his bedroom walls. He dropped his eyes toward the floor and found himself in a city of his own creation.

It was an American (though ornately Old European-styled) city with sidewalk cafés. Black wrought-iron tables, aromatic coffees and teas, raisin-filled cakes on silver trays. Cars (Fords, mostly, from the 1920s to the present) cruised noiselessly down brick streets. The two men, Robert and his father, sipped white wine and praised the movements and lines of the handsome women strolling briskly together – sometimes arm-in-arm – up the walk.

In recent days Robert had made a minor correction: the women now were naked – a natural phenomenon in my splendid city, Robert decided. This new touch greatly improved the tone and feel of the talks with his father.

Usually, before ordering a second carafe of wine, Frederick commented on the architecture, which differed only slightly from one evening to the next. "Robbie, I really must congratulate you," he said tonight. "This city is your best yet. It's Barcelona, isn't it?"

"Almost. I've borrowed liberally from Gaudí."

"Yes, I noticed the corkscrew roofs, the waxlike folds in the granite. The lighting's a bit harsh – too much Texas in your sunset."

"We can adjust that."

"Marvelous. Much better. Of course, I recognize certain design elements from our previous evenings together: the crosswalks that fade in the center of the street, the diamond-shaped intersections. The statue in the fountain is new. Venus, is it? But what's she made of?"

"Chocolate," Robert said.

"Chocolate? Charming. Why doesn't she melt in the spray?"

"I don't want her to," Robert said. "This *is* my city."

"Fair enough. But why chocolate?"

"I like chocolate."

Frederick nodded. "Always did. Remember your little weight problem as a kid? But I should caution you, Robbie, aesthetic choices can't be made on personal whim. I get the impression you're not *thinking through* your projects with enough discipline these days."

"You've always thought that."

"Well – "

"Ever since I returned to representation."

Frederick sniffed. "Sentimental portraits of your mother and your wife."

– which the Old Man, the Master, the Famous Iconoclast who'd helped free American painting from Subject, always held against him. Frederick couldn't abide the fact that his boy didn't demonstrate the passion or the flair for the kinds of daring, monochrome abstractions he'd pioneered in the fifties. Robert was firmly attached to the human form.

"We don't disagree, do we, that art should lance the boil of the set-in-stone?" Frederick said.

Robert laughed. "Lance the boil" had always been one of Frederick's favorite expressions. To him, Conventionality, whatever guises it took – including straightforward figurative painting – was a hideous black blemish.

"Dad, we've trampled this grass to death," Robert said. "Abstraction was a cliché by the time I started painting."

"But there were other avenues you could've explored. Junk-sculpture. Stuffed goats, car bumpers, that sort of thing. The sixties were a fertile lab of ideas. *And* a hell of a lot of fun. You didn't have to become Norman Rockwell."

Robert let that pass. "I'll grant you, abstraction's stock seems to be rising again," he said. "At the Whitney this year – "

"Balls. Dime-store imitations of Pollock and myself. The galleries are filled with stale piss instead of the wine of life." Frederick snapped his fingers. "Waiter! A carafe of your finest piss, please!"

Robert realized that in some cut-rate Freudian fashion he was using these talks to rehash unresolved arguments he'd had with his father over the years. He also recognized that dialogues, stripped to the bone, are power plays, often ugly: the dominant conversational partner sets the subject, tone and pace; the responder adds incidentals, details, counterweight, and heft. These recent discussions with Frederick were agitated both by habit and circumstance. *Habit* dictated that his father dominate. *Circumstance* required Robert to perform Take as well as Give.

"Ruth" and "Art" remained the two most bitter topics between them. "Ruth was too young when she married me," Frederick said in life, and again in these vivid after-death get-togethers. "Your mother had stars in her eyes. I knew we wouldn't last – I was married to my own heroic gestures, as they say – but I didn't want to crush the poor girl."

And on Robert's recent efforts: "You do what you do with great skill, Robbie, but it's merely decorative wallpaper. It doesn't advance the cause of art."

Robert was tired of hearing this. "Screw art's cause," he said. "I paint what I paint because I like my mother's face. I enjoy my wife's honest smile."

And there it was, the *real* trouble between them: Frederick's celebrated inconstancy and Robert's faithfulness to women.

"Vulnerability," Frederick said. "A synonym for 'marriage.' Lance the boil, I say."

Now as always, personal topics gave way to theory as the two men spoke. The people they knew together – Robert's wife and mother – became merely figures, then examples (what to do, what not to do in your lifelong fencing with women), then nothing even remotely identifiable – color streaks in the conversation.

———

Tonight Robert's city was almost Barcelona but it smelled of Cajun delights. Blackened redfish, filet gumbo. Female nudes mailed letters, trotted after cabs, popped open purple umbrellas. Frederick drained his glass and beamed. The ladies in their frank poses pleased him.

Moved by his father's happiness, Robert dropped his guard. "Maybe you're right about my work," he said. "It's probably not as good as it could be. But I've been distracted lately."

"By what?" Frederick ordered more wine. He picked up his knife.

Robert scraped at a mauve acrylic dab on his thumb. "The

truth is, I'm having a hell of a time accepting the fact that you're gone."

"Suffer," Frederick said, and spryly sliced his fish.

On the streets of Houston, Paris, Budapest, and the *real* Barcelona, women, sadly, weren't naked. They wore scarves against the wind, tinted glasses against swirling dust and glare. They wore soft sneakers on the subways, saving their cruelly shaped high heels in plastic bags until they reached the office.

They were harried and tired and angry, hungry, hurtling into or out of love.

This was a world – of concrete, steel, and actuality – that Frederick didn't feel at home in.

"I'm a Romantic," he'd once told Robert. "Romantics never stop believing in possibilities. That's what makes us so appealing – but also, I confess, unfaithful and often irresponsible. We're always running after the next new thing."

A rare moment of candor. Robert must've been twenty-four or five at the time – this was ten years ago in New York, in a hotel bar on Lexington. The subject, then as most often, was why Frederick left Ruth. "My heart," he said. "It's always yearning."

Robert remembered other actual conversations he'd had with his dad, brief moments when the walls were down, the screens of violent color washed clean.

One evening, six or seven years ago, they'd walked to the Village Vanguard to hear Woody Shaw blow golden jazz. Old Max Gordon, the club owner, always hovering at the back of the room; Shaw; now Frederick – all dead, Robert realized with a start. The sights and sounds of a whole era, vanished.

That night Frederick had clucked with pleasure whenever the drummer tickled the hi-hat. He got drunker than usual. After the band's last set he stumbled on the cement steps rising to the street and roughed-up his shins. "Damn booze," he said. "It's made me clumsy and fat." Later in his studio he admitted, "I stare at my canvases now and think, 'This next series'll drive a stake through my reputation.'"

"You've said that about everything you've ever done," Robert reminded him.

"No, this is different. Age, maybe. Or too much whiskey. I worry they'll see what a fake I am."

"Dad – "

"But then I think, Fuck it, I'm going to see it through. I'm going to by God *make it work.*"

And he always did.

Another time, in Houston. They were sitting in a Tex-Mex place on Navigation Boulevard, near the shrimp-stinking Ship Channel. Margaritas, palm-leaf green; piñatas, red-and-yellow paper cutouts on the walls. The day before, the Cultural Arts Council of Houston had commissioned a skyline portrait from the city's famous son. Frederick was nervous about it – normally he didn't work on commission, but this was for a celebration of Texas images, and Frederick was touched to be included. He had a large and sincere civic conscience. Near the end of the meal he leaned over his enchiladas verdes and whispered to Robert, "The thing is, you know, I can't paint the skyline."

"Why not?"

"I don't know *how* to paint figuratively – not really." He looked around the restaurant. "I paint the only way I know. Don't tell anyone."

Eventually he produced a large abstract canvas of brown and orange and gray. *Houston Colors,* he called it. The Arts Council was thrilled.

And then, eight months ago: "I'm frightened of dying," he said.

He'd gone off Camels and Scotch, been through detox. Chemotherapy had left him gaunt and weak. His face seemed to re-emerge after years of sternness, puffiness, lack of sleep. He had high cheekbones, an angular chin, and wide, friendly blue eyes. It was at last a face that Robert wanted to paint.

"Do I look like a cancer victim?" Frederick wanted to know one day. "How apparent is it?" He and Robert were strolling the corridors of the medical center together.

"You look okay, Dad. You needed to lose some weight," Robert said.

"Hell of a way to do it, eh? People are different when you're sick," Frederick said. "You're an embodiment of frailty so they feel they can confess all their weaknesses to you. Total strangers. In the last three months I've heard more about heart murmurs and limp pricks and lost ambitions than I care to mention. How do I look? Really?"

Robert reached to steady him.

"Don't treat me like an invalid!" Frederick wheezed.

Later in the car, on the way to Robert's house, Frederick tried to make light of his illness. Snow fell in cotton-ball bursts from the sky. The streets were icing over. Robert's windshield wipers barely moved; he couldn't see the curves ahead. Frederick suggested they park the car and take a cab. "We don't want to be badly killed," he said.

Robert didn't hear his father's final words, but a doctor later repeated for him Frederick's last coherent sentence. He'd been given a series of disorienting drugs for his pain. The doctors kept asking him, "Do you know where you are? Mr. Becker?"

Softly, and as gently ironic as ever, Frederick answered, "I'm in the lobby of Heaven." Then he'd closed his eyes against the color of the light.

"Nice buttocks, don't you think?" Frederick is pointing across the central square of Almost-Barcelona. "That woman over there by the lamppost, trying to hail a taxi."

"Very nice, yes."

"*She* could be a model."

"What do you mean?"

"I mean if you insist on painting – " His lips curled. "People."

"Can we not discuss my career?" Robert says.

"Not going well, is it?"

"Not at the moment, no."

"Perhaps if you took more risks."

"Precisely what the marketplace won't tolerate."

"Balls to the marketplace." Frederick raises his voice. "I'm talking about – "

"I know. The cause of art. The cause of art doesn't feed me."

"Spiritually or otherwise?"

"You know what I mean."

Frederick wipes his lips with a gold serviette. "So you've taken on graphic design?"

"Temporarily. It helps pay the bills."

"I left you a tidy sum."

Robert laughs. "All tied up in the courts right now. Your dealer, your former dealer, the dealer before that – they each want a piece."

"I see. And you blame me?"

Robert pours more wine.

"Oh hell," Frederick says. "You're not going to be so tiresome as to be angry at me for dying on you?"

No, Robert thinks. I'm furious at the fact of your birth.

Frederick winces.

"I'm sorry," Robert says. "I didn't mean that."

"The truth will out."

"I *am* a bit pissed – "

"Only a bit?"

Robert swivels his shoulders. The tension there cracks. "When Mother died I could've used a little help. She had medical bills up to here – "

"Your mother didn't want my help."

"Oh?"

"She knew where I was. She could've called me."

"She'd never do that. Dignity was all she had at the end."

Frederick shrugs.

"When *you* died, Fay and the others wouldn't have anything to do with the arrangements – "

"Fay's a ninny and a prig." Frederick coughs magnificently, as he was unable to do in his final days. "She stopped speaking to me when I ran out on your mother."

"Lance the boil?"

"What?"

"My engagement to Sarah," Robert says. "That's what you told me when you heard about it, remember? 'A wife is an impediment to a painter. She'll want more money than you can provide her, she'll eat into your work-time.'"

"Was I wrong?"

Robert glares at his father.

"All right, all right," Frederick says. "The wording may have been excessively harsh, but the advice is sound, I think."

At the wedding Frederick shook Robert's hand and said, "Here's wishing you a happy and fruitful first marriage."

Sarah stirs in bed next to Robert. He kisses her shoulder while fixing his stare on a pair of nude women window-shopping at a bakery.

"And these young lovelies?" Frederick waves at the women. "*I'm* not making them up."

"They're here for your benefit."

"Oh, I see. You get no pleasure from them whatso-damn-ever. Does Sarah know what you're daydreaming?"

"Shhh! You'll wake her."

Now all the men in the city, except Robert and his father, are naked. Waiters, bird-sellers, traffic cops. Why not, Robert thinks.

"I agree," Frederick says. "Egalitarianism."

"Dad, I love you dearly but you're a damn scrounge. You're a rotten pork chop."

"No argument from me." Frederick raises his glass.

"I've always wanted to say that to your pointy little beard."

"These recent paintings of yours, Robbie – they're like little plucked chickens from some aborted Grander Design, am I right?"

Sarah snuffles in her sleep.

Robert says, "Okay, enough of this *Bad-boy Becker* bullshit. It may play in the art press but not with me. What we *really* need to cover here – once and for all and let the dead horse rot – is Mother – "

"How I left her with no options."

"Right. And me – "

"How I never encouraged you on your own path. Does that just about do it?"

"No, goddammit! You were afraid my work would be an embarrassment to yours!"

Sarah's eyes snap open in the dark. She moves a bare knee up Robert's leg. "What's the matter, sweetie? Can't you sleep?"

"Just thinking," Robert says.

"What about?"

Frederick rolls his eyes and sips his wine. Mourning doves spin around the bedroom, the busy brick streets.

"Nothing. Go back to sleep. It's all right."

She's already dozing again. Robert smooths her hair. She smells of jasmine – her perfume – soap, heat. This lovely, patient woman, he thinks. This beautiful, beautiful boil.

Frederick sprouts unease. Open displays of emotion – messy, messy, he'd say.

A bus picks up half-a-dozen naked women. In Robert's backyard studio, a splashed-red canvas waits for morning light. He thinks of things to do with his painting, things to cook tomorrow for Sarah; he's eager for the day to begin.

He realizes he's been staring at his father with restless, quaking fists. Frederick watches him slowly unroll his hands. Then the Maestro relaxes, sighs, gazes appreciatively at his son's splendid city. Still too much Houston in the light, but what the hell. The earth-tones, the serrated windows, the statue in the fountain . . .

"Chocolate?"

"Chocolate."

"Charming."

While the Light Lasts

His father's last great work wasn't a painting at all, but a 42 x 80 x 8-inch collage fashioned of steel, wood, canvas, and magnesium. Titled *The Rook's Journey*, it featured a flat, wilted chess rook caged behind bars leaning toward an armored female torso. To her left, a string of wire and nails suggesting a barbed-wire fence blocked her from a rumpled man's shirt (made of metal) with a hole in the heart.

UPS brought *The Rook's Journey*, with seven large paintings, to Robert's door nine weeks after his father's cremation. He was still reeling from the death, though the cancer's certain journey through Frederick's body had long been diagnosed. Months ago, the elder artist had cleared and closed his West Village studio, shipping tables, chairs, and a few blank canvases to Robert's Houston home. Robert's own studio was cleaner and a good deal more austere than Frederick's loft. On Robert's last visit to New York, six years ago, Frederick had joked about the speckled acrylics darkening his windows, walls, and floors. "Looks like I blew my brains out in here," he said. Instead, he'd slowly drunk and smoked away his health – two of the painter's clichés, along with numerous affairs, he'd never overcome.

Robert painted in a square tin shed behind his house, a one-bedroom tract home in south Houston paid for largely by Sarah's teacher's salary (occasionally Robert sold a painting). In the garden by the shed, near an overgrown flowerbed, he'd planted cucumbers. Each spring, wasps dug holes in the soil, down to the vegetables' roots, and pulled out blackflies. He loved the little ritual. The wasps were shiny, with two white spots on their backs. They inserted their stingers into the flies' tiny throats, then cradled them like babies all the way back to the nest.

This busy routine contrasted nicely with the shed's interior calm, the stillness Robert tried to bring to his portraits of Sarah and his mother. He could sit unmoving, studying the teasing shapes on his sketch pads – the way a shoulder shaded up into a neck, the way a muscle seemed to throb on the rippling white space of a page – and still feel energized by the activity in his garden.

Through his window blinds, at different times of day, light changed depth and shape, grew loud then soft like a jazz improvisation, and played across shelves of objects Robert had collected over the years, like treasures in a Joseph Cornell box: a paper-sack cat, two tickets from the Barcelona Metro, a thimble from his mother's sewing kit, a satin cricket in a glass.

He'd installed direct lighting and a CD stereo system in the shed's thin walls. He'd even built a cot, for catnaps during marathon sessions on one or another painting.

The Rook's Journey came to rest on that cot the day it was delivered. Robert hadn't expected it. A storage company, acting on Frederick's months-old instructions, had just caught up with its inventory.

Perhaps the woman's belly – a pinch of prurience – or the violence of the shirt's steel hem lured Robert's eye. He couldn't stop watching the piece.

The paintings held him too, though they were, for Frederick, standard abstractions, variations on his life's work. Unlike Newman and Kline, who'd slipped into easy repetition, Frederick managed to do what he'd always done while convincing his viewers that new discoveries were still being made. These final paintings had that promise of secrets revealed in the very textures of the brushstrokes.

But *The Rook's Journey* was something else entirely, a break with pure abstraction, with paint itself, the smooth oily smell, the sticky skin clinging to canvas like flesh on bone, that had always intoxicated him.

He'd reinvented himself at the end and Robert hadn't seen it, staring at the pale sleeping man in his hospital bed, on his way to becoming a ghost.

Historians, critics, fellow artists would soon cite Frederick's transformation, reassess his career in light of the Rook, arguing the work's final worth – "Becker's Triumph?" "The Failures of Abstraction?" The Vultures of Cultural Value would soon be sifting his ashes.

Robert scorned this debate in advance, though he'd already made the mistake of showing the Rook to Walter Hope, a curator for the Now Arts Museum. Hope pressed for a Becker retrospective as soon as he learned the man was sick. Weak with grief, Robert agreed to a show.

Hope dropped by his studio the day the Rook arrived. He barely glanced at Frederick's farewell oils – "Nice, nice," he murmured, walking past them – but lost himself before the stunning steel woman, the man's abandoned shirt. "This is his?" he whispered. He reached through the bars to touch the sagging castle. "This is Becker's?"

Robert wished he'd covered the piece in a corner by his trinket-shelves – he wasn't ready to share it – but he hadn't thought ahead. Since dawn he'd tried to invigorate his latest portrait of Sarah, a standing nude. Lines and circles interlaced at awkward points, lips and breasts bobbled out of balance. Colors ran, orange, red to blue, but there was no illusion of movement. He was bothered by the heat and the playful shouts of neighbor boys.

Most of all, he was distracted by his father's parting shot.

"And this," he said, tapping his portrait with a dry sable brush. "This is a Becker too."

Hope grinned. "I'll be damned," he said, touching again the giant collage. "The wily son of a bitch." He wore a gray herringbone coat and pleated slacks. Slight squint. Crossed arms. The cool professional pose. "Forty years he hides his feelings with splashes and drips, then he gives us this raw confession."

Robert was annoyed. "What makes you think it's autobiographical?"

"Come on Robbie, we all knew about your dad and, you know – "

"What?"

"Women."

He turned away. He couldn't afford to be angry with Hope.

All the colors of his palette lay beyond his window. Yellow, purple, a smooth buttery brown, blazing now in full noon sun. Rhododendrons, columbines, a few late tulips; the pale icy cloud of an iris, waist-high, above its stalk. Wasps sealed gaps in their nests, to secure the eggs inside.

"The missing heart," Hope said, pacing for different angles, different light. "The shirt like wrinkled skin. And – obviously, right? – the rook's a withered cock. It's all about the loss of his virility." He laughed, then caught himself. "Sorry, Robbie, I'm not ribbing the man. It's the *work*, it's so witty."

Robert didn't smile. He'd formed a first impression of his own: knowing his father's love of puns, he'd immediately grasped that *The Rook's Journey* was a play on Hogarth's *The Rake's Progress*, about a young man's dissolution.

Here was an old rake's tragic end.

"Rook" as "fool."

"This has got to be part of the show," Hope said.

Robert didn't want him looking anymore, especially as he was smart enough to see certain things.

He'd once promised Robert his own show. "When the market's stable. The Japanese are skittish about investing now, and there's a shrinking national arts audience. Best to wait."

Frederick's retrospective would draw record local crowds, he felt, spark the scene back to life.

Once again, Robert would simply be the famous man's son.

"We'll have a third of the museum's space, and I've lined up some miracle carpenters," Hope said. "Chronology's a bore, but I'd like to convey a sense of progress leading up to – " He almost embraced the Rook. "Also, this is Houston, so we want your father's rough side. The more genteel paintings . . . I don't know, I see them displayed in D.C., setting off the neoclassicism there, but here . . . here we want the cowboy, the maverick, the iconoclast."

The heat and this cold dissection of his father dizzied Robert. He wouldn't return to his portrait today. The Now Arts Museum already owned many of Frederick's old works. Hope would arrange a time so he and Robert could go through the catalog together, and assemble, collage-like, the essential Becker.

———

The show's timing was bad for Robert and Sarah. They'd hit a rough spot in their marriage. Weeks passed without a caress or more than an affectionate kiss. Since Frederick's death, Robert had been numb. Insensate, Sarah said. She was patient at first, then restless. Finally angry.

"I can't stand this moping anymore. I need you, Robbie, and you aren't there for me."

"Honey, I can't – "

"You *won't*. I'm living alone here. It's morbid." In bed she pulled his face to hers. Her cheeks were small and round, the color of varnished birch. The skin creme she rubbed into her thighs smelled of lemon. "I'm more naked in your paintings than I am in your life."

She bought Alvin Ailey tickets, tickets to a performance of *Lear,* sexy new dresses, chocolates. Nothing interested Robert.

On their tenth wedding anniversary she went to a styling salon and had her bangs cut. "Eurohair," she said. "It's what all the Paris thirty-somethings are wearing."

"Very nice," Robert said.

She threw down her purse. "That's it. I feel pathetic trying to please you."

Robert reached for her arm. "I'm sorry, sweetie. I'll snap out of it. I promise. Give me time."

"You've said that for months now, Robbie, but every day you're back in that goddamn shed . . . you know, I didn't complain when your father was sick. I fixed lunches for him, went to see him in the hospital. I spent a lot of time with him, and the truth is, that old man never really liked me. He didn't like women."

Robert squeezed her hand. He'd just been painting; his fingers were the walnut brown of her hair. "He liked them too much."

"He liked fucking. That's not the same."

Her remark recalled to him a talk he'd had with Frederick at his wedding. "Sarah's a beautiful girl, Robbie, but she can't be everything to you. That's too much burden to place on one woman."

"What are you saying?"

"A little fatherly advice. I suppose I'm not one to speak." Thirty years ago he'd left for New York, stranding Robert and his mother in Houston. "But here's the truth: show me a man who hasn't picked a hundred flowers and I'll show you a wretch who doesn't deserve the world's bounty."

Always, Robert came away from these talks feeling he was content with too little in life.

The week the Rook arrived, Sarah flew to Seattle for a linguistics conference. She looked forward to this gathering each year, where she'd made a lot of friends. They ate in the best restaurants, spent late nights in their hotel suites telling silly jokes. Like a slumber party, Sarah said.

Before she left she memorized a poem. She had a conference-pal, a lanky New Yorker named Henry Martin, who shared her love of lit. Henry had never seen the virtues of Emily

Dickinson; Thomas Hardy, his hero, left Sarah cold. So annually they agreed to learn a few stanzas by the other's favorite poet and discuss them.

"Stupid ghost story," Sarah said of this year's verse:

He does not think that I haunt here nightly;
How shall I let him know
That whither his fancy sets him wandering
I, too, alertly go? –

"Henry's got his work cut out for him, persuading me this is anything but drivel."

Robert noticed the lift in her voice whenever she mentioned her friend. In the past she'd told him the man was a shameless flirt, but she'd never taken his advances seriously.

This year, Robert wondered if the haircut and the new Talbots dresses had more to do with Henry than their wedding anniversary.

"I love you," he told Sarah at the airport. "When you come back, we'll start over, okay?"

She nodded, kissed him quickly, then ran for her plane.

———

Now she stared at him from his easel. He spread Permagel on the painting's yellow background, an accretion of strokes thick as pitch. She was dead. Color and tone were right. He'd fixed the scale, balanced proportions. Maybe her pose was the problem. Straight-ahead frontal. Passive. A woman being ogled.

Behind him, on the cot, the woman in his father's collage blazed with vital presence.

The sun had baked the shed. He was sweating, dizzy. He picked up his palette knife, thinned Sarah's hips. The neighbor boys, Tommy and Steve, were shouting again as Tommy pulled his little brother in a wagon through the alley. Steve had a coloring book and some crayons. Robert watched them through his window.

Recently he and Sarah had resolved not to have kids. She was a full-time career woman, he was devoted to his art. Robert believed the decision was right for them, but he felt a pang now, listening to the boys, a hollow whistling deep in his chest.

Steve licked a piece of Raw Umber and apparently decided to eat it.

Last week Robert had seen the boys asleep in their yard, on a cotton blanket beneath a pecan tree. He'd sketched their pretty faces, their tight, pink fists, the dragonflies weaving above them. Now, in a stack of paper, he found the sketch: the simplicity of it pleased him, reminded him of his love of charcoals, pencils, and pastels, and momentarily eased his frustration with the nude.

He tacked the drawing next to his painting of Sarah. Could he even imagine babies in his wife's slender body? See her hugging boys like these? Perhaps he was more disappointed than he'd thought with their agreement.

He wondered if he'd cooled to Sarah – *had* he cooled to Sarah? – not when he lost his father, but when she told him, once and for all, she didn't want kids.

He turned away from the empty figure on his canvas, toward Frederick's collage. The woman's torso gleamed like a coat of mail. Now there was a sensual image, he thought. Sexy and inviting. Nipples hard as rivets – lush, bold, *riveting*.

Who was she? Someone Frederick knew, loved, fucked? A young artist charmed by the Old Master? Had he sworn to steer her through the New York art world and make her famous? Had he done it?

How many others had he slept with and promised careers, while Robert languished in the cultural backwaters of Texas? How many women, since Robert's mother, had he pledged his love to?

Robert's head was pounding. He wasn't being fair to his father, and he'd wound himself up so much, the pain in his temples nearly blinded him. Loneliness, jealousy, anger, grief – a narrow range of colors. He needed to relax, as he had while sketching the boys. A simple pleasure, joyous, swift. Wasn't that what Frederick meant at the wedding? Grab the world's gifts?

Women were the presents Frederick always gave himself. Easy to condemn, but (Robert thought now, content with too little) what was wrong with that? Before he met Sarah, he'd had only two serious love affairs; since his marriage, he'd been faithful to his wife, but Sarah had no right to tell him what to feel, or to demand total attention from him. He was hurting, goddammit, childless and forgotten as a painter – while his father moved on, *played* out his life. And became the better artist for it.

The torso in the collage: it wasn't one person, Robert saw now – it was a lifetime of women, a passionate engagement with their thoughts, words, buttocks, and ankles, their startling laughter and sighs, their lustrous sexuality – an abundance Robert hadn't allowed himself, and now wished he'd explored.

"Art," Picasso said, "is never chaste."

———

Superman rang.

Robert had moved the Rook to the floor and fallen asleep on the cot. His sweat soaked the pillow. He switched on a portable fan on a table near his shelves, then reached for the phone. The receiver was an eight-inch plastic replica of the Man of Steel. It had been on sale in the Galleria at an incredibly low price and Robert figured what the hell, as long as it works. He felt powerful, speaking to people while gripping all these muscles.

"Robbie, hi, I wake you?"

Hope.

Robert had been waiting to hear from Sarah. Not a word since she'd left for Seattle. He'd tried her hotel room several times in the last three days.

"The grand Becker," Hope said. "The biggest, most arrogant canvases from each decade. How's that for a theme? Fits Houston perfectly – the brash young city erupting out of nowhere, competing for world dominance with its oil wells, money, and swagger. Where *else* could your father have come from?"

He wanted Robert to meet him at the museum tomorrow morning to help arrange the show. "And bring that beautiful Rook-baby, right? You'll need a truck or a van. I'll send someone to pick you up, say nine?"

Robert's head was thrumming again. He felt heavy and chilled, as if shoved into a swift-running bayou. "I need more time," he said.

"Nine-thirty."

"No, I mean . . . I'm not ready for this. It's too soon, Walter. It's ghoulish. The man's barely dead, for Christ's sake – "

"Robbie boy, I'm going to let you in on a little secret," Hope said. "If we don't make a positive statement now about your father's work, his enemies – the enemies of abstraction – will seize the initiative, brand him as a has-been, and that'll be that. Frederick Becker will disappear from art history."

A fever, damp and yellow, lodged behind Robert's eyes.

"You hear what I'm saying? Aesthetic values, individual reputations – how do you think these things are made? Your father knew, Robbie. It's political warfare. You better get with the program, man."

Hope was Robert's best shot at a museum show of his own (though painting was passé with the hot young crowd Now Arts tended to promote), so he backed down, agreed to bring the Rook.

"Good man," Hope said.

Robert hung up the phone, swallowed a couple of aspirin, then tried Sarah's room. No luck. He left a message with the desk: "I love you. Please call me."

Off in a golden bower, he thought, whispering third-rate poems to her lover.

He approached his portrait. Technically, it wasn't bad now but it still inspired nothing in him. Frederick had once said of Robert's work in general, "Striking a balance between having something real at issue and a wonderful surface isn't easy, but you have the second, now go back and introduce the first. Art, we said, is a grid superimposed on another grid – both things are necessary."

How like his dad! The formal tone, the royal "we" as if he were God the Father and the Son of Man all in one!

Robert challenged himself: what *was* at stake in this latest picture of Sarah? My desire for new sexual experiences, he thought. No wonder she didn't dazzle.

Where was she each night? In Henry's room? Thomas Hardy and sweet little nothings in her ear? He was probably overwrought again. Maybe he was projecting his own restlessness onto her. Or maybe at heart she also regretted their decision, and felt their sexual life had come to "zero at the bone." If so, maybe a fling with Henry was just what she needed. Would Robert deny her that comfort?

His earlier certainty that promiscuity fed the fires of art struck him now as silly. He laughed at himself. "Promiscuity." Even his thoughts were shy. In word, if not deed, he was as formal as his father.

He couldn't imagine himself courting another woman. He wouldn't know how to begin. *Want to see my sketches?* And the women he'd loved before Sarah – they were happily married now, model mothers. When he'd known them, they were wild and confused, impulsively lustful, convinced that attention from Robert – or any man – was the only measure of their worth. They both told him, when they left him, he was "too nice," as though they didn't deserve tenderness and respect. Since then, they'd each tried Freudian therapy, and emerged from it healthier, more assured, capable of sustaining good marriages and raising children. Robert was happy for his old friends, but when he spoke to them now on the phone, at Thanksgiving or Christmas, he heard the price they'd paid for progress. They sounded dull, strident in their maturity, drained of sexuality. He'd seen the best women of his generation destroyed by psychoanalysis.

"There's no such thing as progress – in life or in art," Frederick said at Robert's first gallery reception, in '79. He'd raised a glass of wine to toast his son's future. "There's only adding-on."

Robert stood now and added a few strokes to Sarah's belly, a red highlight to her hair. The oil on his fingers smelled vaguely of her sex; surely a mental trick, a manifestation of his need to *capture* this woman.

What if he blurred her calves, abstracted her a bit?

Giacometti saw women's bodies as towering trees.

He tried, and failed, again to reach Sarah in Seattle. She must know she was driving him crazy, and this angered him all the more.

Wasps and early fireflies circled his tulips. He heard Tommy and Steve's mother calling them in to dinner, her voice as smooth and resonant as a wind chime.

He dropped a sheet on the Rook for tomorrow morning's trip. His headache shrieked. He was about to betray the piece. After all, bad light filled the museum. And stupid crowds. They were a threat to his father's work. They didn't love art, Robert thought; they craved art world gossip. He imagined them at the opening, gulping wine, nibbling pale crackers smeared with brie. His father would share the space with scorched genitalia made of paper, framed subway doors covered with graffiti, human hair in shopping bags – the latest in "statement" art, though the only statements being made, Robert thought, were that violence sells, and that his peers' imaginations were a bizarre mix of Pee Wee Herman and Ivan the Terrible.

Here the Rook was safe. The shed was like a greenhouse, warm and enclosed. To fully thrive, an imaginative object had to be watched over time. Its meaning or effect *moved* with the viewer's emotions, with temperature and lighting. Hope would never understand, but Robert decided he had to live with the Rook one more day – to engage in an intense relationship with it, morning, noon, and night, the way his father did with women – and feel the many ways it changed him.

MORNING

Robert drew his blinds against the harsh and glary dawn. He stood in the middle of his shed with a fresh cup of coffee. From this distance, the piece seemed welcoming and soft. The background was pink and tan with a slight hint of yellow. A smoker's sallow flesh.

He stepped closer. The narrative was clear. A torn, bloodied shirt reached hopelessly for a very young woman. Heavily shielded, emotionally cold, she had ripped out his heart, left him limp, like the rook.

Frederick rarely spoke of heartbreak, loss or regret; his last years might have been lonely. Robert didn't know.

By midmorning, in stronger light, the shirt looked mean and hard, grabbing for the woman, who had softened. Robert saw a small tarnished streak on her belly, the color of skin. A break in her armor.

Or a Caesarean scar – a reference, perhaps, to Robert's birth. The narrative shifted, and he saw his mother threatened by the swaying, drunken shirt.

She was small, thin, and quiet. Early in her marriage, against her wishes, Frederick spent late nights in Houston's "colored" clubs, listening to Erskine Hawkins, Peck Kelly, Woody Herman, and his favorite, the great jazz drummer Big Sid Catlett. He and his friends were often the only white boys in the place, but they truly loved the music so they were welcome. Frederick claimed later he learned all he knew about freedom of gesture from these brilliant, inventive musicians.

But his nightly escapades shattered Ruth, who never fully recovered from Robert's difficult birth. She grew weaker, nursing her baby, while her husband was God knows where. Twenty years later, as she was dying of breast cancer, she told Robert she wished she'd had the gumption then to kick Frederick out.

("I wish," said Joseph Cornell, the day he died, "I had not been so reserved.")

She never understood why Frederick married her.

Robert learned the answer one night in New York. He was just a boy at the time, eleven or twelve; he loved his summer visits back east because his dad spoke to him like a grown-up. The black women in Houston's R & B clubs were "mighty fine," Frederick told him one August. "Sweet-smelling, like roses, and silky. Friendly as hell. You'd walk into one of those places, some lady'd kiss you, put a cold beer in your hand, and say, 'Sit with me, sugar.' Dark and mysterious, like someone had turned out a lamp in her, leaving a sexy silhouette."

Eventually the club-girls lost their exotic aura, he needed something different, something special, and Ruth, a white woman raised in Africa, fit the bill.

She was the child of Baptist missionaries in Lagos. She didn't see America until she was twenty. When Frederick met her in Houston, this young café waitress was unlike any woman he had ever seen, timid but self-possessed. She resisted his slickness at first, and entertained him with stories that later de-lighted Robert as a boy – about the python that dropped from a date palm onto her father's pulpit one day, the deep-throated drums she fell asleep to each night.

She told Robert other stories once Frederick had moved to Manhattan. She'd pop a thimble onto her thumb, busy herself with buttons, and frighten Robert with tales of his father's wild nights, his verbal cruelty. She seemed powerful, describing these events, almost regal in her mourning. One evening, sad for his mother, lonely for his father but terrified too, Robert crawled into her lap while she was sewing. She lost her balance in the chair and nicked his hand with her needle. The bleeding stopped quickly but he wouldn't quit sobbing until Ruth phoned Frederick in New York and he heard both his parents' voices, assuring him everything was all right.

Frederick's Village studio was large and gloomy; its shadowy corners scared Robert as a child, and so did Frederick with his massive build and goatish beard. Once, he caught Robert cry-ing in front of a violent red abstraction titled *Self-Portrait*, and asked him what was the matter. Robert repeated Ruth's charges. Frederick laughed, hugged his boy, and said, "Don't confuse the monster in the paint with the monster here beside you. And don't listen to your mother."

He didn't drink before six. In the afternoons he'd take Robert to neighborhood fairs, or to watch the chess players in Washington Square Park. He'd dance with young women at block parties, give quarters to raggedy men on the streets, praise the stickmen he'd seen at the Village Gate or the Five Spot. Back in his studio, he'd show Robert how to hold a paintbrush, how to make a vanishing point on the canvas, using a picture he'd taken of the Ramblas on a visit to Barcelona. When Robert finished his first portrait, a copy of the photo, Frederick handed him two torn tickets from the Barcelona Metro. He'd kept them as souvenirs, and gave them to Robert for a job well done. At such times, Robert felt immense love for this man. He wasn't the ogre Ruth had described. He was vital, fascinating, funny. And he *belonged* in New York. Even as a kid, Robert knew the city's rhythms, its walking spaces, suited Frederick more than Houston ever could, though the City of Heat always held a special charm for him.

He *did* change when he drank. He'd rage at his paintings as if they were people he didn't like. If Robert interrupted him, he'd snap, "What do you want?" then apologize.

Now and then he'd nod in grudging kindness at a mark he'd made on a little stretch of canvas.

Robert learned to dread the fall of night, the *crack* of a Scotch bottle seal. Shadows lengthened in the studio's grim corners. But in the morning, Manhattan was once again a circus (cab fumes and pizza smells, laughter, women, store-front displays) and Frederick an amiable clown.

NOON

The light softened behind tall blue Gulf Coast clouds – a lull before the blast of full day.

Robert, wearing only cut-off jeans, ignored the phone as he leaned into his painting with an extra fine brush, dabbing pearls into the nude's dark hair. She'd just walked out of the sea.

He no longer thought of her as Sarah. Ruth was there, too, in the pale legs, the vulnerable stance, though this was neither his mother nor his wife. He'd smudged her face, so personality, history, emotion wouldn't shape his lines or choose his colors for him. He focused now on texture, the seductions of density and weight, inviting the viewer to leave the world and enter the frozen grace of paint. The figure was approaching a clarity he liked, but with a gentleness he remembered from Monet, the cool dappled shadows of the Giverny paintings.

Superman jumped in his cradle again. It might be Sarah, but Robert feared Hope was trying to track him. On the other hand, if he didn't answer, the man might storm his shed later on.

"Robbie, I need you! Where the hell are you?" At first it sounded like his father, shouting from a near distance, and he knew he'd been haunted all day, like the man in the Hardy poem Sarah had left by the bed:

*. . . he goes and wants me with him
More than he used to do,
Never he sees my faithful phantom
Though he speaks thereto.

But it was only Hope. Robert explained he was learning
from the Rook – techniques, new ways of seeing; he needed to
keep it a while.

"We're ready to go! The opening's next week. We can't wait."

They argued further until Hope finally said, "I can help you,
Robbie. Remember what I promised?"

Robert thought his skull would burst. It was suddenly clear
to him: this asshole was going to string him along forever.

"I can get you a show. That's what you want, isn't it?"

"Of course." Robert's hand began to cramp and he loosened
his grip on the brush. He hadn't realized he'd worked so long
today. Hope didn't care for his portraits – the man was just trying to get to Frederick. His pledge was a cynical bribe. "Look,
Walter, you've got the paintings. Pick them without me,"
Robert said. "The Rook stays here for now."

He hung up and immediately regretted the damage he'd
done. Hope could deliberately mount a weak show, tarnish his
father's image.

He started to call back but dialed Seattle instead. Ruth and
Sarah – his portraits – stared at him from the walls of the shed.
The collage was like his father's presence in the room. Robert
grew dizzy again. Cicadas throbbed in the pecan tree next door.
Tommy and Steve's mother was humming a tune, watering her
fat tomatoes.

Sarah answered the phone.

"I don't believe it," Robert said.

"Robbie! I was about to call you." She sounded out of breath.
"We've had trouble with the phone in our room."

"Right. No one's there to answer it."

"It was broken. Have you been trying to reach me?"

"You could've called me from a pay phone."

"I'm sorry. It's been so hectic. You know how it is at
conferences."

He *didn't* know. "How's Henry?"

"Fine."

"Did he convince you the poem was a gem? Maybe late one night in his room?"

She laughed, nervously. "Have you been into the booze?"

Robert never drank; she knew that. He picked up the bottle of Anacin. He'd been eating the things all day.

He said, "Are you happy, Sarah?"

She was silent. He heard the woman next door singing "Strawberry Fields Forever." Linda? LuAnn? She was pretty – and young for a mother of two. Robert realized he'd never seen or heard a man over there.

"Sarah, would you like to have kids?"

"You've been sitting around brooding in that awful shed. We settled that. Didn't we?"

"I don't know."

"You're having second thoughts?"

"Maybe."

"Oh Robbie . . . is this serious? Do you really want to open this up again, because if so, it's not something I can deal with on the phone – "

"Are you sleeping with Henry?"

As soon as he asked this, he knew he was really afraid, and he couldn't stop pressing her. Maybe it was the fever or the aspirin or both. Or maybe he'd sensed the truth.

"I'm not even going to answer that," Sarah said. "You're the one who stopped sleeping with me, remember?"

"So you run to – "

"*You* must've strayed. Why else would you accuse me like this? I don't even know who I'm talking to." Robert heard tears in her voice. "*What's going on?*"

"I love you."

"I love you too, Robbie."

His head seemed to thicken, like quick-drying glue. "Are you also in love with Henry?"

"For God's sakes, no!"

He stood inches from the woman on his canvas, glaring at her unprotected breasts. "Are you sure?"

She tried a lighter tone. "Let's stop this, okay? My flight arrives Friday at – "

"Sarah."

"Goddammit, you want me to sleep with him? Is that what you want?" She fumbled the receiver. "All right, yes, I've spent a lot of time with him this week. He's sweet. A lot sweeter than you've been lately. Jesus, Robbie, it's like you *want* to drive me away . . ."

"I don't want that. It's been a difficult period."

"For me too, all right? Yes, yes, I enjoy the attention of a man who still finds me attractive. I'm sorry about your father, Robbie, I truly am, but *I'm* not a ghost. I'm still here and I have needs."

His knees wavered. He had to sit. He'd never felt so unsure of himself. The doubts had begun the day the Rook arrived. It was the source of all his anxiety. His marriage, his talent, his lost parents seemed as elusive now as the collage's shifting narratives. He couldn't grasp anything, and in his desperation, he couldn't stop the pain he knew he was causing his wife.

"I'm up each dawn painting," he told her. "I want you to call me tomorrow morning at five. From your room. I want to hear your voice first thing – maybe it'll help me do good work."

"That's three Seattle time, Robbie. I'm not going to get up in the middle of the night."

"If you don't call me, I'll know you're with Henry."

"Jesus, what *is* this? What's gotten into you? We're married ten years and you're giving me a test?"

"Call me."

"I will. But not at three A.M."

"All right, then."

"Robbie, don't take that tone with me. Listen to yourself. Do you hear how crazy this is?"

"Dawn, Sarah. I'm up at dawn." He nearly snapped his receiver in half.

"Henry's a lot easier," she said, and cut their connection.

———

Naked and sweating, he turned the songs up loud: McKinney's Cotton Pickers, 1933, with Big Sid Catlett on drums. Sid was known for his swing, a freer time-keeping style than most of his contemporaries played. Kicking and prodding bass drum and snare, he accented the solo lines of piano and horns.

Free-style swing. Robert wondered if he had it. His father certainly did. He stared at the Rook. The music lightened the woman, the shirt. They were caught in a giddy dance. The red setting sun cast a raw erotic glow on the floor.

Robert walked into his garden, shooing wasps from his head. His hair was tousled and damp, his face on fire. He'd eaten all the aspirin. He moved like a sleepwalker.

He picked cucumbers, radishes, greens. A few flowers. In the kitchen he whipped up a salad and a light vinaigrette. He showered, dressed. The fact that he didn't *know* the woman next door, not even her name, occurred to him briefly, but he was floating, free of gravity and social convention.

He poured the salad into a nice wooden bowl, then snatched the paper cat from his shed. His father had made the animal years ago, when Robert was a child. Perhaps if he offered it to Tommy and Steve, their mother would be pleased.

He didn't ask himself what he'd say when she came to the door, or what he intended to do. He *was* self-conscious enough to go around back, through the alley.

Webworm silk drifted like lace in the branches of the tree. Pecans – and a plastic soldier – crunched beneath his feet. He was buoyed by the music in his head, the mint smell from the woman's herb garden. The air cooled his fevered skin.

He tapped on the sliding glass door. Steve laughed at something in the living room. The woman, in a T-shirt and jeans, smiled in recognition when she saw him. They'd waved a few times across the fence. She stepped onto the patio.

For a moment he didn't breathe. "Hi, I was in my garden, and I thought you'd like – "

"Oh, how sweet of you," she said, taking the flowers and the bowl from his hands. Her short dark hair smelled of lilacs, her skin the warmth of vanilla.

Sweet. Sarah's word for Henry. He gave her the cat. "For the kids."

"It's lovely."

He'd start with her mouth: at first, just a fine, dark line to center the face, then a dab of Alizarin Crimson . . .

"Scott and I've meant to have you and your wife over," she said. "We're just, with the kids and all, our schedules aren't easy. I'm Lenore."

"Robert."

A man called from the kitchen, "Honey, who's that?"

Robert's stomach clenched. He caught a glimpse of his own fiery cheeks in the sliding glass door. He looked like shit.

"Lenny, honey, let's go," the man said. He sounded like Frederick when Robert was little. Whenever Frederick wanted something he'd shout, "Robbie, I need you. Get over here. Let's go!"

Lenore shrugged. "We were just out the door. The boys, you know, McDonalds."

"Sure."

"We'll enjoy this later, though. It's really nice of you."

Her smile nearly knocked him over, onto sharp, ripe pecans in the grass. "Wait a minute," he said, thinking quickly. "Don't move. I'll be right back."

He ran through a tangle of ivy in the alley and thought again of Giverny: Monet's dense, cluttered greens, a sensual paradise.

He picked up the Rook and lugged it back next door. "I want you to have this too," he told Lenore.

She placed a hand on her throat, looked curious then nervous. "It's so large. I couldn't possibly . . . what *is* it?"

"A gift. Take it. Take it, please."

Her husband poked his head out the door. He was blond and fair. "Lenny – "

"Scott, honey, this is Robert." She spoke carefully. "He lives next door."

Scott started to shake Robert's hand then saw the naked torso. "Whoa. What the hell have you got there?" he said. His lip twitched as though he'd just tasted something bitter and hot. "What the hell are you . . . who *are* you?"

"My father was a very famous man," Robert explained. "This piece is worth a lot of money."

Scott laughed – a short, angry burst. "Right," he said.

"I've decided I can't have it around. If you don't want it, sell it. The museum – "

"We can't . . ." said Lenore.

"Listen." Scott glanced at his wife then slowly shook his head. "I don't know who you are or what the hell you're doing, hauling this . . . this *obscenity* over here – "

Lenore gripped her husband's arm. "No, honey, he was – "

Robert saw the confusion on her face. He thought, *What have I done?* She turned away from the stark metal breasts. "I'm sorry," he said.

Inside, the boys screamed for Quarter-Pounders. Scott said, "You keep your sicko stuff away from my kids, hear me? I don't want them seeing crap like this."

Robert tried again to apologize to Lenore but she wouldn't look at him and he didn't know what to say.

In the shed he stripped once more and cursed his mother's face. If she hadn't been such a *princess,* so enamored of her suffering, if she'd humored Frederick, followed him to the City of Art – how different Robert's life would have been! He'd have seen the shapes his father saw, learned the joys of women.

As it was, he couldn't do a decent picture of his wife or even talk to the lady next door.

He threw the empty Anacin bottle at Ruth.

The goddamn collage! Perfect in conception and design, filled with slippery puns: Duchamp. His famous chess match with a nude young woman.

Robert was the rook, torturing himself with the work. He'd call Hope tomorrow and have it carted out of here.

Big Sid rumbled all around him, floor tom to cymbal to snare, a fanfare fit for paradise. Monet's Eden was free of people – an ideal condition, Robert thought. "Leave me alone!" he shouted at his walls. He tore an old sketch of Ruth into shreds. Her eyes, her lips, her teeth fluttered to the floor. He slammed his hand on his desk. A sharp lance split his palm; he pulled away. A wasp had flown through his window and landed where he hit. The pain made his hand cramp again. He thought of his mother's sewing needle, the voices of his parents when they were both alive to soothe him.

The warm J & B seared his throat. Only a damn monster could drink this stuff.

He'd never painted drunk. Frederick used to say whiskey slapped him awake. Robert decided to try it – nothing else had pricked his imagination – though he didn't know if his swollen hand could hold a brush.

His mind crackled with fever and aspirin and booze.

On his knees he picked up his mother's parts. Her chalky skin smeared his palms. He clapped to clean them, wincing from the burn of the sting, and continued to clap, sitting by the Rook. The grand Becker. Bravo.

Woozy, he crawled toward the woman. She stood before him like a dare. He licked her steel-plated thigh.

He whispered his mother's name, then his wife's, over and over like a poem. Solid, familiar sounds. Sounds of comfort.

He reached for the metal shirt. His father's last trace. Where had the material come from? Part of a car door, an oven, a corrugated roof?

For a moment his anguish changed to wonder at his father's gift, as it did so often when he was a kid in New York. Frederick had taken what the world didn't want, a tossed-off scrap, and fashioned this image, nearly human.

An act of salvation, which moved Robert deeply. Rescue, redemption. A confession, Hope had called it. The piece seemed to touch him now with a quiet, abiding grace.

In the low evening glow, the woman was whole again, strong and assured. The shirt looked beaten and flat. Poor bastard, happy only as long as the light lasts.

Let him reach, Robert thought. Let him believe in possibilities.

He got to his feet near his easel, skin against paint, and ran his fingers over his portrait. "Come home," he whispered. The woman had no face. "Please come home."

Overwhelmed by his fever and the heat, he tumbled onto his cot. The scents from his garden, musky and sweet, reminded him of Frederick's R & B women, their rose perfume, their smoky mysteries like the textures of dreams. He didn't move all night (except once, when he thought he felt a warm, steel finger touch his face), and was awakened by Sarah's call.

Three

Akhmatova's Notebook: 1940

A drayman in an oak wagon offers me a ride to the square. On cloudy days, not much light, I still look young.

"Where are you going?" he says.

"To the prison."

"What for?"

"My son," I explain.

"Arrested?"

"For the second time."

"What's he done?"

I've made him nervous. "His mother's a poet."

"Is that so?" He flicks the reins; his horses shiver. "Maybe I know you."

"I don't think so."

"No, really, what's your name?"

"Akhmatova."

He looks at me. "Anna Akhmatova?"

"Yes."

"I was sorry to hear about your husband, Miss."

"Thank you. This will be fine."

Outside the prison, women in black shawls stand one behind the other.

"Come to the tavern with me," says the drayman, trying to be cheerful. He pats the wagon's seat. "You can sit here under the feather blanket while I buy you a beer."

I thank him for the ride.

"I'd like to hear a poem."

I smile, shake my head, then take my place in line. The walls are scratched and gouged. The woman in front of me turns and asks, "Can you put this into words?"

I tell her, "I can."

Women whisper that they bleed beneath their skirts. In Petersburg the men, in a hurry, won't listen. Instead they hear a clamor of crows, the bell of the gray cathedral. Irritable, quiet, I pass through their rooms, dreams replacing dreams all night.

Lena, I ask you again: Who can refuse to live her own life?

Lately I've dreamed of you as a child in your long white dress, trampling the wild-onion dirt in the hills above town. "He looked at me funny, Anya." "Well, his brother touched my hand." "Does Father pull your drawers down when he hits?"

When we were small I refused to wear white dresses so that people could tell us apart.

In one of my dreams Mother's talking again about the city of Kitezh, saved from the Tartars by prayer. "It was lifted straight into Heaven, just beyond those hills," she says. "On days when the fish are still and all the mud has settled to the bottom you can see its reflection in the lake. Each man had a wagon. Their wives raised many, many children."

You follow her pointing finger to the tip of one bald peak. Softly, to me: "She's telling it wrong."

"Why? What do you mean?"

"It wasn't saved. It was just a city of brides. Their husbands had gone to war."

"What happened?"

"The Tartars raped and murdered all the women. Left only bones."

"How do you know this?"

"Riga" – a girl in our school – "told me."

Mother buttons her sweater. "It's getting colder. Let's go home now." She takes my hand.

Rubbing your arms in the mist you warn me, "One day, Anya, we'll live in Kitezh."

———

Dry snow, candlelight mirrored in a stranger's dining room window. First course (served in silver dishes by a dour maid): roast duck with apricots, cranberries, a light Gewürztraminer. Next, mushrooms in lobster sauce, cream gravy, Jarlsberg cheese. Coffee and chocolate for dessert.

Afterwards we sit by the fire. The rug is soft and warm.

"I could treat you to meals like this every night," says my host. He ships vegetables and fruits around the world, acres and acres of foodstuffs.

"And what would I have to do to earn them?"

He laughs. "Nothing. Enjoy yourself."

I shake my head. "I *did* enjoy this evening. I'm glad you invited me."

I'd seen him at the market earlier this week, supervising a dozen crates of Jonathan apples unloaded from a Dutch steamer.

"I'm not the first to ask you," he says.

"I'm comfortable living by myself. Choosing my friends."

"And your lovers? There must be several men."

I smile.

"Poor bastards."

"I don't lie to them."

"Food's going to be scarce in the coming months – the army will need it. I can help . . ." he says.

"Thank you, no."

"Tell me then."

"What?"

"How do men kiss you?" He lifts my chin. "Tell me how you kiss."

Lev is thin. Black bread and sugarless tea. I appeal to the authorities on behalf of my son, but my voice, in chorus with dozens of other women, is indecipherable. Day and night in the dank pine waiting room, the smell of mercurochrome, swabbed across the corns on our feet.

I've been a bad mother. When Nikolay first proposed marriage (he was cocky as a prince), I told him I hadn't the patience for courtship; I wanted to sit by the Neva, reading *Hamlet*.

"So you want to be a poet," he said. "What are you going to write?"

"I don't know. Whatever interests me."

"Pretty odes on wind chimes or cats?"

"Of course not. Why are you being so hateful?" I turned toward the river and opened my book.

He shook my shoulder. "Have you ever heard rifle fire? A young soldier moaning and clutching his guts in a field? My God, Anna, what do you know of the world?"

"Enough to tell you no," I said. "Leave me alone. Go be a man."

The following day he took a holiday train to France with six other young army recruits. Three weeks later I heard he'd swallowed a vial of strychnine. For nearly a day he lay unconscious in the Bois de Bologne before a young couple stumbled upon him. Three times he threatened suicide, twice I refused to marry him. But it turned out he was right.

A witness to one's time, Lena. What else is a poet but that?

When Lev was born (October, mild and warm) I discovered how little I possessed of the simple love by which people live day to day. Working for each other, eating together under the same roof. Nikolay spent half the year hunting in Abyssinia. I read my poems, shouting over drunks, in bars.

Our son grew up in his grandmother's house, eighty kilometers east of here. I didn't even visit.

"I want to see Kitezh."

"Don't." I pleaded with you to put your skirt back on, and to come away from the lake.

"Mother's wrong."

"Please, Lena."

"Someday . . ." You gazed at the waves.

"We can make our own city," I said.

"What do you mean?"

"In the sky. Or under water."

"With nasty boys?"

"And rich, spiced food."

You smiled, pulling on your socks. "All right, Anya, you start."

A priest stops me outside the prison. "Good woman, come pray with me."

"I'm not a good woman," I tell him. "Besides, there's no one to hear."

Five or six rabbis also wait outside the gates.

"Of course there is. We each have an angel – "

I laugh. "I'm a descendant of Eve, Father. Read your Bible." I lace my boots up tight.

"No forgiveness for those who won't seek it!" he calls after me.

In the bars, men sat at my table and swore they loved me. We discussed art about women, women as artists. One night Mikhail, a painter friend of mine, said, "Feminine beauty is an imperative." He couldn't afford oils; I often gave him lipstick to mark his large canvases. "It tugs at my hand when I pick up the brush."

"Romantic nonsense."

"No no," said another. "It's the serenity I'm interested – "

I slapped the table, spilling beer. "Listen to you. All of you. Have you ever really *seen* a woman?"

"We've offended poor Anna."

"Here, have another glass," the men said.

"You don't even *begin* to know – " I pulled a cigarette from a pack and leaned toward a white candle stuck in a bottle's mouth.

"A toast to Anna," Mikhail teased. "A magnificent, fearsome woman."

"Listen to me – " I said.

"To Beauty."

"To Art."

"And to bed."

For many years after you'd gone (ripples flattening out; gas pockets in the mud, the sulfurous steam; bats whirring in the bushes) I resented you. And Nikolay, volunteering for the front, leaving me alone here in Petersburg. Even when the Bolsheviks murdered him I felt nothing but rage for my husband. Lev had just turned ten. I was drunk and loud each night in the Wandering Dog.

"The wasteland grows." For a time, early in our marriage, Nikolay liked to puff himself up and quote European philosophers, to impress me.

"What do you do on these hunting trips when you're not hunting?" I asked him once. "Play cards? Go to brothels? What do men do on their own?"

"Why?" he said.

"I want to know, that's all."

"We drink. We laugh. We talk."

"What about?"

"Money. Philosophy. Your friends at the Dog aren't the only ones with thoughts in their heads."

"What kind of philosophy?" I asked.

"The future, the world, that sort of thing." He pulled off his boots. I massaged his feet. "The other night at dinner, Peter was telling us that Nietzsche – Peter's favorite – has a wonderful definition of mass violence – or, as he calls it, the True Twentieth Century."

"What does he say?" I asked.

" 'The wasteland grows.' "

"That's it? 'The wasteland grows'?"

"He wrote it in 1880 – or '90, something like that. Before the war. Before Verdun, the Somme . . . he was a prophet."

Nikolay never noticed the paradox until I pointed it out. "Waste makes barren, limits, opposes growth," I said. "How can a wasteland grow?"

He stared at me.

Years later, cleaning out his things, I understood the answer. The wasteland grows, spreads like a swamp, if we forget to remember.

––––––

When the Wandering Dog burned down, the poets and writers of Petersburg scattered, each like Lear without his kingdom.

Cigarettes, candles, amorous dancing – an accident, said the police. "Wild bohemian artists," they called us. "Pimps and whores."

Most of my friends stayed silent or quietly left. Now I sit by the Neva and wonder what they'd say about our city? Flat, white buildings, haphazard construction, the squalor of the market. Increasing numbers of soldiers on the streets. All this talk, from travelers, about the Reich's frightening power in Germany.

The wasteland grows.

––––––

"She's famous. Why doesn't she say something on our behalf?" "It's because of her fame that her son is in jail." "She's no better than the rest of us."

The women's hushed voices echo beneath the pine wood ceiling. Lev lies, in a half-stupor, on the cold cell floor. I cup my palms beneath the spigot in the courtyard, run quickly back into the prison, but by the time my hands reach his lips there's nothing left to drink. "Lev, Lev . . ."

Fame is so much water.

Today I can't afford both dinner and a beer. I buy a squash, hurry home and toss it in a pot on the stove. Start some tea.

Early in the morning the men arrived . . .

They came at dawn . . .

At dawn they came . . .

While the kettle whistles I write this sentence, tear it apart, make it again, slightly new.

―――――

Polonius, to Hamlet: "What do you read, my lord?"

"Words words words."

―――――

A visitor from the West.

"I'm afraid I have only boiled potatoes to offer you," I tell him.

"No no, nothing for me, thank you." He settles uncomfortably into my armchair. Pillows stretch across the floor. Your picture, Lena, in a silver frame on my desk.

My guest's card (he helps me with the English) reads: Mr. Alfred Weller, First Secretary in the British Embassy in Moscow. He has requested this meeting with me out of admiration for my work.

"You've just returned from Paris?" I say.

"Yes. I have news of some of your friends." His Russian is awkward; I stop him and ask him to repeat. "Aleksander Halpern, Pasternak, Shileyko – they're all doing well. Modigliani has become quite famous since he died."

"Really! When I knew him he'd dig and dig in his pockets and never make the price of a drink." We laugh. Mr. Weller watches me closely. His eyes are small; he hasn't much hair.

"They're very concerned about you, your friends. Every day we hear more rumors out of Germany. War seems inevitable."

The tenant below noisily unlocks his door. We glance at the walls.

"Would I be any safer in Paris?"

"At least you'd be among friends. You could publish." He stares appreciatively at my ankles.

"I couldn't leave Petersburg now. Old habits and all. I can hardly bring myself to say its new name. Leningrad. Cold and official."

"Do you have any recent work I can take to your colleagues in Europe?" asks Mr. Weller. "They're eager to see what you're doing."

I turn on my desk lamp. "As a matter of fact, I've just started a long poem – the first in nearly a year. It's dedicated to the women who wait with me outside the prison."

"Yes, I heard about your son. I'm sorry."

I glance at the page. It isn't about my son. Truthfully, I haven't thought of Lev in days. "Do you find me attractive, Mr. Weller?"

He fidgets with his coat. "Of course," he says softly.

"Don't." I read him the first lines of the poem:

> At dawn they came to take you away.
> You were my dead, I walked behind.
> In the dark room the children cried,
> the holy candle gasped for air.

I ask him, "Can you follow the meaning?"

"Yes," he says.

"These words, these little scribbles, Mr. Weller, are all that matter to me. More than your admiration. More than the prison. Or my son."

"You don't mean that."

I sit. "Sometimes . . . sometimes after working I feel that way."

"Then by all means come to Paris – where your poems can be seen."

"I don't approve of emigration."

He makes a little gesture with his hand. "If you'll forgive me, Miss Akhmatova, I think your stubbornness is misplaced. It's all very well to die for one's country – "

"Dying *for* one's country is easy," I tell him. "Dying *with* it is another matter entirely."

"We have to make it easy for people to walk," you said.

"Light and shade. Cool spaces for babies."

"I'm not going to have any babies."

"Oh, Lena, of course you will."

"If it's a boy he'll grow up and leave you. Girls you never get rid of."

"I'm not going to live with Mama all my life."

"She's a stupid woman," you said.

"No she's not."

"Wrong about everything."

"Like what?"

"Everything."

"See, you can't say."

"She shouldn't let Father hit her. And the lake. She's wrong about the lake."

"Riga's the one who doesn't know anything."

"The streets have to be wide enough for horses and carts. No automobiles. Absolutely no automobiles."

"Maybe one or two?" I said.

———

I walk in a field of factory ash with only my shawl and a hairful of snow. My books have been burned in the square.

This morning Lev's face is bruised, his lips are chapped and torn.

"What did they do to you?"

A dry cough. "Stop it, Mother."

"Don't strain. Quietly."

He lifts his face toward mine. "They put a bag on my head. A bag of water. When they kicked me, my nose and throat filled till I thought I would drown. I couldn't stop choking."

I stroke his sweating back.

"Who was it?" he says.

"What are you talking about?"

"In your apartment."

"When?"

"'As long as she entertains men in her apartment,' they said . . ."

He closes his eyes. His long black hair comes off in patches on my hands.

———

Not, not mine: it's somebody else's wound.
I could never have borne it. So take the thing
that happened, hide it, stick it in the ground.
Whisk the lamps away. . . .

———

"Bowls," Mikhail said in the bar one night. "Jars. Glazed china plates."

"Even the word 'containers' is a conceptual burden placed on women," I said.

"You take yourself too seriously, Anna."

"I object to not being seen."

"Men create these images in order to praise women, don't you see that? Angels. Swans. Damp, dripping caves – "

"You might as well be papering a wall, to hide what's underneath." I snuffed the candle to punctuate the point.

"Delilah with her scissors . . ."

———

Just after we married, Nikolay and I traveled to Paris. I remember thinking, "These streets have leaped from my mind," I felt so at home. I imagined the city of Kitezh looked something like this: women walking freely, laughing, in their light skirts and stockings.

In his quiet room Modigliani sketched me in pencil, the slender lines of my neck shading off into plumes.

One afternoon on my own (Nikolay and I had already grown restless in each other's company) I walked through a refurbished neighborhood on the Ile de la Cité. The sky had been dark all day; as I passed a laborer setting buckets of brown paint in the window of an unfinished apartment, hail began to patter the awnings. The laborer invited me inside. The apartment, he said, had once housed happy men, but they had all gone.

"Where did they go?" I said.

He seemed not to hear. "Where are you from? You don't look French."

"Petersburg."

"Ah, the noble peasant. High plains? Sheaves of wheat?"

"Well . . ."

He laughed, and tapped my finger. "A very pretty ring. Do you have any children?"

"No," I said.

He was quiet for a moment, busying himself with his rags.

"My wife is in the clinic, expecting our first child," he said finally. "Twenty years old, my wife. I'm quite a bit older, as you can see."

As he spoke he cleaned his brushes in a little can of turpentine marked "Flammable." His hands were long and explosive.

"I haven't gone to visit her."

A piece of hail, like a heavy crystal wine glass tossed at the sill, tipped a half-empty bucket onto the waxed wooden floor. The man didn't move. Brown paint seeped into the cracks beneath the carpet; his child waited in a place without color.

"I don't know what to do," he said.

"What do you mean?"

"All these years. I didn't know a woman's body could be so huge."

"Hippogriff, mermaid, manticore," Mikhail said. "Siren, sister, witch." Words words words. Crumbling wall, paper (a floral design) sagging to the floor, stretched across the rug like a dress dropped in haste. The naked animal herself out the window, on the canvas, trembling at the edge of the page. To a nunnery, in a winery, passed out on the dirt. Container and contained. In Pushkin's land.

Mr. Weller requests another chat. On the phone I tell him no. "The Party's asked me to write a poem praising Stalin."

According to all reports, he says, the Germans are murdering hundreds of thousands of Jews.

"Why the Jews?" I ask.

He doesn't know.

My days are a series of nonmeetings. Admissions of nothing. The roomer below is afraid to meet me on the stairs.

"Brick towers."

"No no, Lena, wood." I laughed and pulled your hair.

"Brick is solid, Anya. We want our city to be solid."

"Well, *my* city's going to be pretty and smooth. Lots of wood. And copper."

"I'd rather be safe."

"Wood's safe."

"Not from fire."

"There won't be any fires in our city. We'll run them out of town."

"We'll have the best firehouse in the world."

"With six gray horses."

"And three fat men."

———

The bats we discovered as children still squeal inside the cypress trunks. Remember how they frightened our aunts?

The day you finally went looking for the city of Kitezh, Mother and her sisters sang hymns from the Bible. As minnows rose in the shallows near the trees they praised God's love to me. "You have the gift of words, Anya," Mother said. "Use it for His glory."

Father and Uncle Svetan basted the calf's hind legs: shallots, crackling butter. "Are the children hungry?" Uncle Svetan asked.

"Where's Lena?" said one of the aunts.

"I thought she was with you."

"No, she – Oh my Lord."

They gathered at the water's edge, in knee-deep mud (gas pockets popping all around them), trying to call you back. The meat began to burn.

This evening I can't see the lake: no moon. But I know where it is. I can hear it. The news from Paris is bad. Men say, Lena, that all of Europe may fall to the German attack. Russia, too, perhaps. My friends urge me to join them – next month they're sailing to America – but "someone," I write Shileyko, "has to be a witness."

Bats echo in the hills. I walk back to town. Two soldiers with rifles on their shoulders leave a house by a darkened side door. Someone's crying in the kitchen; I duck down the street. A young woman carrying a child in a burlap sack sniffs around the empty market stall where I'm hidden. Rotten peach halves. Scattered apples. She scrubs the dirt, hands a grapefruit rind to her baby.

"No," the child protests.

"Eat, *eat.*"

Fresh graves and bread crusts end another day of commerce.

Lev will be released in ten days. The prison official smiles at me. "No more guests?"

"No," I say.

"The Party, I understand, was quite pleased with your tribute."

A young wife, waiting for news of her own, squeezes my hand. Across the room, other women – tired mothers – glare at me.

I stop by the market. Cabbage is all I can afford and still have the price of a drink. Tucking the small head under my arm I treat myself to a beer in a tavern not far from where the Wandering Dog once stood.

In the apartment, still holding the cabbage, I fluff my pillows, straighten the Modigliani in its cracked brown frame. My eyes have faded a bit. With a towel I dust the table before setting the cabbage down.

From my window I see draymen returning from the fields, milk cans clattering, empty, in their wagons. Children menace each other with sticks. A couple of soldiers pass in the street. "Keep me company tonight?" one yells up at me. His friend laughs and bumps into two old women, knocking the frailer one to the ground. She spits. The soldier scolds: "Watch where you're going. Crazy old bitch."

The world will never want us. I know this. I'm going to tell everyone.

"Did you love my father?" Lev slouches over cabbage and boiled potatoes. His second day home – too weak, until this evening, to speak.

"I felt sorry for him. Would you like another potato?"

"Yes. Why? What made him so pathetic?"

"He wasn't pathetic. I never thought that. It's just that he wanted – what? To be a great man, I suppose. First as a philosopher, then as a husband, a hunter, a soldier. He used to tell me, 'I was born for these things.'"

"Was he really a traitor?"

I stack our plates on the counter. "He was killed because of his poetry."

"That must have increased its value."

"His spare style, the Bolsheviks said, 'betrayed our rich Russian culture.'"

"And you?" The color has returned to Lev's cheeks; his back still aches. "Don't you want to be great? A great writer?"

"Yes."

"So I should feel sorry for *you?*"

"The way I see it, people's judgments are beyond my control. Your father couldn't accept that."

"I suppose I've helped your career."

"What do you mean?"

"Jail. Your loneliness. Your terrible suffering – all that."

"Hush."

"I'm sure you've written about it."

"No."

"Then you will. It's too good to pass up, eh? And who knows – a poem here, a poem there, perhaps I'll wind up in prison again."

I dry my hands. "I'm sorry, Lev. I never intended my work to affect your life this way."

"But it has, hasn't it? Maybe I should get myself killed. Then you'd surely be great. The Great Akhmatova." He stands, painfully. "Where was she until I wound up in jail?"

"You knew where I was. You could have come to me."

He tosses his cup onto the pile of dirty plates. The cathedral bell rings once, twice, twice again.

———

A small steamer's anchored in the river. On board, dozens of young soldiers, crisp in their belts and boots; crates of fruit. Women clutch rosaries near the now-empty market, whisper prayers, wave at the boys as they pull away in the boat.

"I hear that your son is home again."

I nod to the woman beside me.

"Thank God. You're very fortunate."

"Yes," I say. "I am."

Such grief might make the mountains stoop,
reverse the waters where they flow,
but cannot burst these ponderous bolts
that block us from the prison cells. . . .

This evening it's clear to me, Lena: Mother *was* wrong. What we see in the lake is not a reflection of Kitezh, but the city itself. Marble columns, cobbled streets, fish rounding corners, quick as light.

The True Twentieth Century: I've finally lived to see it. I drop my shawl on the bank, remove my shoes and skirt. The water is cold. Pinnacles, vaulting, an Ogee arch. Stained glass, crockets engraved with ball flower designs. Rotting wood. Straight ahead, a white gate: is this the way in? You can tell me.

Yes, I hear you whisper. Or maybe it's the water swishing. Louder now, yes: *Closer, come a little closer . . .*

Here I am. My lungs begin to ache. No, I think. *Closer, Anya, come this way . . .*

No. My place is with the dying, not the dead.

I surface, catch my breath. My skirt, a purple patch, waves to me from the shore.

In town, merchants fold their awnings. I shiver, shake back my short wet hair. A light goes out in a window. This is how the world ends: acquiescent, Lena. Peaceful. No help needed from us. I sit by the Neva and laugh. My pretty fool, my lovely foolish home . . . I've forgiven everyone. You'll be my angel now.

THE OBSERVATORY

September 1, 1987: Claire's latest letter, postmarked Jerusalem, begins: "We've learned a new trick, a process known as oral rehydration. Last night Azziz and I, with the help of some UNICEF folks, administered salt-and-sugar packets to several pairs of parents, for their kids. My pet projects – birth control, literacy – have sprouted wings. Still, the Mighty Penis rules our group and I've said so. A few of the men, including Azziz, are beginning to listen. In the meantime I'm amazed at the resiliency and resolve of the women over here. They have a real country-toughness, though windstorms and war have forced most of the rural communities to fold up their tents.

"So now we depend on city-dwellers for support. They clothe us, offer us food and shelter. Of course we're in constant need of cash. A steady supply comes from sympathizers in the States, but the mails are slow. We're on the move a lot.

"You know what I miss? Woody Allen movies. Has he stopped being funny? Do you get into Houston or Galveston much, or are you too busy wishing on stars? Silly William. Have you found a job?

"You wouldn't know me. I'm whippet-thin, strong (though I'm smoking again). The old devils have started to stir – a couple of girls in our outfit have traded 'meaningful' looks with me, but so far I've kept my hands to myself. You're the last one to've pushed my button.

"Be careful, Will. You may be asked about me."

———

My clearest memories are of intimate moments, such as seeing Claire naked for the very first time: the delight that she was so feminine (I'd had no doubts, yet the sight of her unwrapped brought relief as well as happiness: A woman's body, I said to myself, something with which I'm familiar, and even to some degree practiced). The susceptibility of her skin; the offer; the vulnerability; the variations (breast size, wrist size) from the standard American beauty; the discovery, by watching her gestures and learning their urgency, of what she most (inexhaustibly!) welcomed –

Crazy, recalling all this now – she won't be back. Remember, instead, that blue double star in Lyra earlier tonight: an elongated object to the unaided eye, but when magnified, the pair – *both* blue – stood at least twelve degrees apart. The loveliest things I've seen since Claire, and of sufficient visual interest to record in my log . . .

———

11/23/87. I try to concentrate on the sky but I'm still thinking of C. For five months now, ever since she left, I've collected her letters here in this binder, next to my sketches of Jupiter's gray and yellow bands, Saturn's rings.

Her remarks of October 2 share a page with the Martian polar caps as they appeared in my 'scope last night. What is she becoming? By her third strident paragraph I no longer recognize the person I knew:

". . . more and more women are cutting loose, placing themselves in adversarial roles to their own societies. In the States, it was all I could do not to be enraged every day. The stares of young boys. The sexual compromises. I resent the fact that I was made to feel I had a crisis on my hands if I lost an earring or discovered a run in my hose. . . ."

In this same notebook I scribble replies, only some of which I mail. I'm surprised at my own anger. Often I find myself writing *about* her as though she had died. Sometimes I forget that she's not here.

She'd lost patience with forecasts, proofs and signs. Tossed my atlas aside. "I'm thirty-eight years old, William. *Thirty-eight years old,*" she said.

I continued reading as I'd always done (philosophy, gardening, the lore of star names), hoping to impress on her a sense of continuity, but nothing mattered to Claire after she'd lost the baby.

"There is a view of life which conceives that where the crowd is, there also is the truth," says Kierkegaard. "There is another view which conceives that wherever there is a voting, noisy, audible crowd, untruth would at once be in evidence." I followed the latter principle, gathered my instruments and built my base out of town.

Watermelons, beets, basil and chives, squash, cauliflower, radishes. A deep, sweet water well (the water is heavily fluoridated, comes out of the ground that way, good for the teeth though it stains). I'm self-contained out here, northwest of the city, but discouraging activity surrounds me on all sides. Last month a mobile home park opened up down the road, with huge mercury vapor lights diminishing visibility in the southeastern sky. Crowds in the evenings, curious about my buildings. A mile to the west, bulldozers clearing six acres for a car dealership.

The owners of the mobile home park want more space. They've offered to buy the surrounding lots, but so far the local landowners – including my father, who maintains the three or four acres I occupy – refuse to sell. Meanwhile, migrant families from the east, from the industrial midwest, keep arriving, jobless and violent. Tread worn thin beneath their trailers, cotton towels waving off sun and dust in the windows of their trucks . . .

Like Claire before she left, they're not sure what to think of my place. Of necessity (I didn't, and don't, have much money) the design suggests frustration, dead ends, lack of fulfillment. Made with materials found at various county dumps – bed frames, soup cans, rusted pipes, drilling bits, aluminum foil, TV antennae, tractor tires, a ship's compass, engine blocks, fans, filters from washers and dryers, busted chunks of billboard – the buildings are both functional and full of surprise. The telescope sits in a cinder-block room, round, two-and-a-half meters high. Stones with filed edges. On top, a white pyramid (easier to construct, using loblolly pine, than the more traditional dome).

The optic tube is irrigation pipe taken from a fallow field. Scraped clean. Mounted on a tripod. Carefully, I've calibrated the distance between primary and reflecting mirrors, ground glass like cornmeal on a stone, and balanced the whole assembly with milk cartons full of cement.

A base, in these fractious days, from which to view the world.

Sometimes now on hot afternoons a group of five or six young men, angry at not finding work, sit in front of their house trailers, drinking beer. At a certain point in their shared misery they break out automatic pistols (easy to purchase in

Texas) and use my pyramid for target practice. I've been patient, hunkering down inside, protecting the telescope. It maddens them that I won't show myself. They know I'm here. "Come out, you son of a bitch!" they shout.

Bullets rip through the pyramid's peak.

Lately I've been fighting back, disconnecting their car batteries while the men are asleep, short-circuiting the wires so the mobile home park goes dark. Moonlight on the Airstreams, no wind, whole families bereft of air conditioning trundle out onto the ground – undershirts, nighties, coolers of beer. They take up awkward positions in rickety lawn chairs and try to sleep. I'm sympathetic; they were misinformed. "Lucrative Sun Belt, shit," they say. But they'll have to leave my pyramid alone.

Total lunar eclipse. Temperature in the forties. Slowly, a red shadow moves across the craters, spreading like a cherry stain.

In the fields, grass stirs. Animals nuzzle each other for warmth.

When the shadow recedes, and the moon resumes its stare, cows, milk-thick, greet the day royally before learning it is false.

What's your view like, C? Here, at this time of year, the sky is most receptive when you wake to it in the middle of the night. It's as if a fog has cleared. The constellations have abandoned the positions they held when you first went to bed, the night is chillier, quieter. Giddy now with a plucky, pleasant wind.

Oh, the deep satisfactions of the amateur astronomer: groggy as you pull on your socks, then two or three shirts (for it is cold, very cold, and that's just the way you want it). Wrapping a wool blanket around your shoulders, fixing instant coffee, consulting the atlas. The book smells of last night's dust. It lies heavily in your lap, weighted with mystery: the grainy, cobbled path of the Milky Way, the amoeba-shaped Magellanic Clouds, the star-names in swirling script.

Then you push open the pyramid doors.

A puff of wind. Skin tightens. Genitals recede into the corduroy folds of your pants, coffee turns flat and cold all at once.

But the sky is swimmingly active; it draws you out as power-fully as a sea's undertow.

With shivering hands you open the atlas on the floor, hold its pages with the thermos, and flick on the flashlight. M 20, the Trifid Nebula, is the object of your search tonight. Once you've located it in the book, you must turn off the light and wait for your vision to adjust to the dark. The freezing touch of the telescope's eyepiece startles you. Jittery stars, settling down now . . .

Nothing.

The pages of the atlas are white, the sky is black. The con-trast confuses your ability to calculate angles of position. After several more attempts with the 'scope, you find and center the prize: a blue, crablike cusp of cloud with a pink tinge at the top. Stars golden all around it. By now, the seams of your pants have frozen. They catch the hairs on your thighs. Goosebumps cover your skin. You have good character. You understand discipline. You are mathematically precise and full of bad coffee.

Dedicated.

An amateur.

———

Last night I reread your letters: "No more selfish pursuits." "The individual doesn't matter." "The group is all that counts."

Claire, consider: Do my buildings make sense by them-selves? Can the atlas put its own information to use? No. With-out me – my poor, individuated consciousness – there is no correlation between one thing and another. No rain leaking through the roof. No spider in the corner. No one to lift the flashlight.

———

"I've discovered that, for most men, politics is a matter of ideology," Claire writes. "For women it's the body. We're trained since we're young to use our physical selves. Naturally it's our asses (and not just our thoughts) we lay on the line."

———

12/8/87. Good news, Claire, I *have* found a job. Four nights a week now, for five dollars and twenty cents an hour, I change the light bulbs at the Chemtex Refinery in Baytown. Six thousand, four-hundred ninety-nine light bulbs on fourteen smokestacks, twelve storage tanks, two distillation towers, two cokers, one hydrocracker, eight security gates. At ten o'clock, carrying boxes of fresh supplies, I pace the parking lots searching for burnt-out bulbs. Flames curl from metal kilns; puddles of gasoline and rust reflect the fire and bright filaments. Sulfur, steam, hydrocarbons, nickel, and vanadium mix with gas, skunks, dillweed, sunflowers, and rubber to produce an odor at once sour and sweet. Tonight, climbing the steel hull of the cat cracker, I can see the refinery flames, blue then white then gold, mirrored in the bay waters lapping in from the Gulf. Leaning forward on the ladder, I unscrew a bulb and replace it with another. Flat, metallic air burns the back of my mouth. Hundreds of petrochemical plants surround the bay, their flares like signal fires from distant camps. Rusted ships, broken barges, abandoned loading cranes stand in the shallow water.

From here my pyramid is indistinct, a white smudge lightly shaded by tangles of mesquite. To the south, and to the west, Houston, Galveston, and their suburbs.

———

Christmas eve, light snow: Clinging to the cat cracker, balancing my box of bulbs, I reread with amazement Claire's latest letter: "Our group is changing its tactics, becoming more aggressive – which matches my *personal* growth," she writes. "Today I learned about persuasion. Azziz showed me what to do. First, you pack about a kilo of Cosmopolitan B explosive into a round metal container and build a wooden box around it. Leave a square hole at the top so you can insert the detonator and the fuse. If you want to make it waterproof, you can wrap it in a couple of plastic garbage bags. Secure it with chicken wire – an irregular shape, like it's an old rock lying in the road. Spread some wet cement on it, sprinkle a few pebbles here and there, a little grass and dirt. And that's it. You can rig it to a regular twelve-volt car battery. We'll use it in a march we've planned for next week. Set it off in the street, to disrupt traffic."

The bulb by which I'm reading goes out with a pop. I replace it with a sixty-watt. Headlights snake around the rim of the Gulf, then bunch together at sharp bends and bridges.

Exxon, Arco, Mobil, Shell, Phillips – each plant is a city, self-contained: pulsing, blinking, shimmering in the black bay, lighting the smooth steel bellies of the 747s overhead.

Claire continues, "I don't want you to get the wrong idea about my new buddies, Will. They're not much different from the folks I met in the Peace Corps – dedicated to genuine social change. I've learned, though, that in this part of the world, violence is often the only way to get 'official' attention. So we've radicalized our methods. For all its good will, the Peace Corps will never make a dent in oppression. Nothing short of cataclysm is ever going to help the poor over here. I see that now.

"My colleagues have known these things all along. They aren't crazies, as most Americans think. They're intellectuals of the highest order, very serious and honest, well-read.

"At thirty-eight, I'm the oldest member of the group. Sometimes the women are as bad as the men – they pamper me, as though I'm arthritic or senile or something. They're all in their twenties. A few teenagers – some with kids. I ask them, 'Where are the old ones?' 'Ours is no occupation for drooling old fools who're settled in their ways,' they say. I argue but they don't listen. I understand that my value to them is largely symbolic: a citizen of the world's most privileged nation who's 'seen the light' and thrown her lot in with the poor. They don't expect me to be useful in any practical way. But I intend to be. I can use my symbolic nature to trigger change. All I need is a plan, an explosive public event. Last night I figured one out . . ."

———

C? Are you kidding me?

My hand trembles. Her letter rattles. I read the line again.

Martyr.

The word, like the thought it embodies, intimidates, is somehow unmodern. She writes, "I want to draw the world's attention – I mean the damned television audience – to the needs of displaced women and children. If I have to die to do that, well okay."

A couple of cans of kerosene, she says. Matches or a lighter, she says, "on a day when there's no other story to distract the three major networks."

C. C. C.

A complete lack of irony, if not guile. No regard for personal limitations, or the vast indifference of nations. Masochistic. Why am I attracted (have *always* been attracted) to this side of you? In anyone else it would seem dogmatic, belligerant, foolish.

In myths – remember the stories I read you? – heroes and martyrs walk among the stars. The night sky is filled with those who've triumphed or failed, spectacularly: men, women, and animals who used the planet before us – who bequeathed to us the misery of making choices . . .

———

The first time we made love, Claire asked me to hold her hands above her head, as if they were bound, in bed. Afterwards she was angry at me for complying. I was only trying to please you, I said. Tell me what you want.

———

Sometimes I invite Dalene out to the observatory – she's the Chemtex secretary I mentioned in my last letter. Early twenties, very cute, blond hair hiding her face.

I show her Mars and the moon. When we make love, her expressions of pleasure are loud and prolonged.

I've told her all about you. "If you don't mind me saying so, this Claire lady sounds like a loon," she says. She takes my hand. "Stick with me, William. You're much better off."

Of course she can't figure me out the way *you* always did. "You don't *ever* go into town?" she asks.

"Just to the post office and the bank."

"Too dangerous? Too big?"

"I had to look away."

I open the pyramid doors: Houston, twenty-six miles to the south. Streets circling one another, no tangents. It looks like the failure of knowledge.

———

Gunshots. A wildcatter (I surmise this from his gleaming steel hard hat), drunk and unemployed, sits in a lawn chair in front of his mobile home, aiming a pistol at my pyramid. Wood-chips fly all around me. I crouch behind the 'scope.

―――――

1/8/88. Claire: yesterday, a man named Macon and a man named Leeds asked me about you. I thought you should know. Twice a month I catch a ride into Houston with one of the Chemtex drivers, to deposit my paycheck at Texas Commerce Bank downtown. Macon and Leeds – local FBI – met me in the lobby. I agreed to talk to them when my business was done.

I'd expected them. I knew they'd been reading our letters.

They drove me in a black car to a nearby Ramada Inn. A room on the second floor. From the window I could see a piano propped on a yellow pole in front of a music store.

Bears and Vikings on TV. Macon handed me a beer. "Do you know Ms. Dillon's whereabouts?" he began.

"No." I sat on the bed.

"You've written to her."

"I write back using her postmark, but by then she's usually moved on," I said. "I have no idea whether she gets my notes."

"She left the Peace Corps?"

"Yes."

"Do you know when, exactly?"

"No."

He glanced at a bio sheet on me. "Unemployed for eight months . . . now you work at Chemtex for what . . . five bucks an hour?"

"Five-twenty. I've offered her a small amount for travel expenses, if that's – "

Macon waved his hand. "You're not under investigation here, Mr. Keller. We just want to keep track of her. She wrote you first last July, care of your parents. Is that correct?"

"Yes."

"And your parents forwarded the letter out to your . . ."

"It's an observatory," I said.

"You live there now?"

"Right."

Leeds poured himself a Heineken. He and Macon, stocky

men, both wore dark brown suits, thick, though the weather was warm.

"How would you characterize your relationship with Ms. Dillon?" Leeds asked me.

"Friends. We're friends."

"Are you in love with her? Forgive me for being so personal . . ."

"I was."

"Is she in love with you?"

"I don't think so. Not anymore."

Macon walked to the window and watched the freeway traffic. "It's indiscreet of her to write you. Why would she write you?"

"We spent a lot of time together."

"Was she content – I mean, generally?"

"She chain-smoked – kind of nervous," I said.

"Employed?"

"Cashiering, mostly. At bookstores, restaurants."

"Any violent tendencies that you were aware of at the time?"

"No."

"What did she say about her plans when she left?" Leeds asked.

"She didn't have any."

He checked a page in a folder. "It says here that your father – a realtor in town? – owns the land you live on, is that correct, Mr. Keller?"

"It's been in my family for years," I said.

"What do you do out there, with the telescope and all?"

"I look."

"At what?"

"Things that move. Things that don't."

"William – may I call you William?" Macon said.

"Go ahead."

"William, of course you realize what this is all about."

"Yes."

"But I'm wondering if you know that eight different law enforcement agencies worldwide, including the FBI, suspect Ms.

Dillon's foreign comrades of first-degree murder, in connection with an October ninth bombing in Tunis?"

Murder? I shivered. C. C. C.

"Do you think Ms. Dillon could ever be involved in – "

"I don't know," I said. Claire?

"All right, William," Macon said. He buttoned his coat. "That's all. We'll be in touch."

They'll be watching me, C. Reading my letters to you – do you receive my letters? Five so far – six, including this one. Before I close, let me add, at the risk of attracting prying eyes, that as of eight o'clock this evening, a six-hundred-foot ground cable extends from my fuse box to the edge of the Big Thicket. The limbs of the pines have been wired in honor of your recent resolve. The moment you strike the match (wherever you are – Greece, Turkey, the Middle East – whatever you may have done) I'll throw a switch and a burst of red light will bounce off the water in the bay. In its brilliance the display will eclipse the mercury vapor lights of Houston (one hundred and sixty-five thousand in the downtown area alone), Galveston, Baytown – as far away as Huntsville. The famous prison rodeo held there each year will be suspended until the furious Brahma bulls regain their sight. Planes will be dazzled in the sky.

Admittedly, the meaning of my gesture (love, grief) will be missed. Despite its public nature, mine is a private act.

So, in a way, is yours.

––––––

What are the thoughts of a person about to be set on fire?

When people still believed in Hell, the sight of flames must have startled them even more than it frightens us now.

Do people still believe in Hell? Do you?

Where will the event take place? At what time of day? Will you light your own match or will Azziz do it for you?

Broad outpourings of sympathy the hoped-for result, once the horror has passed.

––––––

One night I woke to find Claire weeping into her pillow. "What's the matter?" I asked.

She said she'd felt impure since her pregnancy. "I want to be loved."

I combed her hair with my hands. "You are, you are," I said.

She sat up and wiped her face. "Did you know that in certain parts of the world, parents believe that babies who don't survive their infancy automatically become angels?" she asked me. A waitress named Linda, an active Pentecostal who worked with C at the restaurant, had been lending us spiritual guidebooks ever since the miscarriage. "Angel Princes of the Altitudes, Angels of the Hours of Days and Nights. They're universally worshipped."

"Let it go, Claire. Please, sweetie, we've been through this. It wasn't your fault," I said. "Maybe it's all for the best. I know it's hard to see that now, but money's tight – "

She rose and tore a sheet of paper out of my notebook. On it she scribbled angel-names. Michael, Gabriel, Raphael.

"What are you doing?" I said.

"Love spell. It's in one of Linda's books." She laughed – "it's just a game" – then taped the page to the cinder-block wall above my pillow. The paper clung loosely to the stone, threatening to fall. "You won't be able to sleep now without thinking of me."

"I'm thinking of you, honey. You're in my bed."

"But I don't know where your mind is."

"I love you, C."

"I know. Hold my wrists."

––––––––

"Yesterday a Palestinian woman approached me in a square," Claire writes. Lebanese postmark. The letter has taken a month to reach me. "Azziz had attached a pipe-bomb to the French ambassador's limo (a warning only – not much punch) because the night before, in an address to Israel's Knesset, he said Europe's children would sleep better at night if our group stopped impeding the humanitarian efforts of Western governments. I led the woman out of the square, to a safe spot several blocks away. She asked me who I was, what I was doing in the Middle East. When I told her I'd come to save her children, she laughed. 'Here, the women have no wombs,' she said. 'What do you mean?' I asked. 'Babies die as babies, or as young soldiers . . . our poor withered cunts are open graves,' she said, and spat a wrinkled prune seed onto the street."

Mobile home kids have trampled my squash. The car lot is encroaching. Claire continues: "As for you, silly Will, I'm worried – out there all by yourself. I agree, American cities are hideous, but isolation isn't the answer. You could choose exile, as I've done.

"The mind does funny things when it's left alone to feed on itself. Get into town. Ask your girlfriend – Dalene? – to take you to the movies. God, what I'd give for a movie . . .

"Or go roller-skating. Play softball. You'll dwindle away to nothing if all you do is *watch.*"

The pain of steady seeing . . .

If, as Sartre says, consciousness is an insatiable hunger, then those who wake at night and turn their eyes toward the hard-to-find are starving.

Insomnia, sensibility (that is, uneasiness at finding oneself in the world) struggling for clarity of expression.

Wretched instant coffee.

Stars as round as cups and saucers.

Tonight my mirrors glisten in the light of the quarter moon. Nebulae, as delicate as a young girl's aureoles, grace my lens. Slight kiss of a crisp wind. A candle burns on a table next to the 'scope. Taped to the pyramid's warm inner wall, a slip of paper – Lévi-Strauss: "What I see is an affliction to me, what I cannot see a reproach."

On my fourth cup of coffee tonight (my thirtieth birthday, alone), I decide to sculpt the lights in the trees, the ones I've arranged to flash on in tribute to – in sorrow over – your self-immolation.

Setting down my thermos, I scale a thin pine and rehang the Christmas bulbs I placed here last week. No pattern in mind, but Form, limited only by the number of lights and the shape of the woods, will sooner or later suggest itself. Nothing as obvious as an insignia, stripes, Star of David, stylized fork-and-spoon which your commando friends have adopted as their symbol. ("We drop them – little paper cutouts – in the name of the world's hungry children, wherever we go," Claire writes.)

Variations on a structural theme, balance, off-centering: a few of the ways to proceed. But my favorite (employed in putting together the observatory), because most challenging, is to eliminate, as I go, individual parts of the construction.

3/15/88. "The postmark's misleading. We've tightened our communications network, so we'll be even harder to trace.

"I'm here in ――― to join the crews of cargo flights chartered by the International Committee of the Red Cross. They don't know I belong to an alternative political organization. They think I'm still with the Peace Corps.

"Anyway, I'm studying the ICRC's methods so we can become more effective; unfortunately, they've got troubles of their own. The C-147s they've chartered belong to the Nigerian government which, until recently, has loaned the planes free of charge as long as they were used for relief efforts. Now the Nigerians have decided they want five thousand dollars per run, a minumum of eight runs a day. The ICRC can't afford it. In addition, some of their food has been sabotaged by armies eager to counteract any Western influence. Our group opposes the economic motives of capitalistic governments but approves of government agencies designed to aid children. It's a contradiction but we live with it.

"I've been in Christian cities, Muslim cities, Buddhist cities. Cities strafed by gunfire. It's exciting, Will. I've sunbathed topless in Tunis, on the roof of a building two blocks from Arafat's stronghold.

"I miss Dr Pepper and (never thought I'd say it) *People* magazine. I haven't fallen in love."

Poverty and oppression naturally feed rebellion. All right. But it's not at all clear to me, Claire, why terrorist acts erupt in one area and not in another, or why a middle-class American woman wants to involve herself in the violence.

Because you had a miscarriage? You fell out of love with me? (She met some people at the "Soup Bowl," where she worked. Old Peace Corps volunteers. On their advice she made a plane reservation. This much I know.)

"The movements of small particles in politics as in physics often deny any explanation" (Walter Laqueur).

Physicists now admit that the smallest particles in the universe are even smaller than they thought.

6/5/88. "I'm feeling sad these days. Melancholy. My time's so short. I told Azziz about my decision. He thinks I'm brave. He'll be my 'stage manager,' in charge of the kerosene and the matches. We figure Thanksgiving is the prime time to do it, when the emphasis in America is on eating. I have five months.

"I kissed one of the girls – one of the teens in our group. It's been a long time. That summer, after I met you, when I wasn't sure I wanted to commit myself to a man . . . since then, I haven't touched any women. Until now. I liked it, Will. I'd forgotten how much it excites me. I was going to practice celibacy over here, hone my mental strength, but . . . it's so gentle with women. No thrusting or pounding or feeling held down. The male body is such a *forward-moving* . . . well, no wonder so many men equate sex with force.

"I like your twinkling trees. It's sweet of you, Will, to commemorate my sacrifice. I miss you. I miss your gaze."

Rewiring the lights: though bulbs like these are usually reserved for Christmas, the holiday effect is strictly to be avoided here. I have no hope of making a statement with a simple string of lights – I'm merely attempting to show solidarity with you.

You'll go up in flames.

I'll light the leaves of the trees.

Do you remember how dense the swamps are, C? In the heart of the woods, surrounded by barbed-wire fences, steaming ponds thicken with chemical paste. PROPERTY OF U.S. FEDERAL GOVERNMENT, signs say. KEEP OUT. Once a place for backseat lovers in beat-up Chevies and Fords, the Thicket's swamp areas are now a breeding ground for crocodiles and birds who've fed on toxic waste since birth, and are immune to it. Yellow swamps, red swamps, black swamps. The heat and light of the nearby refineries bore through the woods. Mist swirls in front of my flashlight whenever I come out here at night to wire the trees. The ground sucks at my shoes, bulbs clink in the bag on my back.

Last night I heard a rustling in the high grass next to the tree I was climbing. The pasty swamps curdled and popped, the sky burned orange with refinery smoke and fire. Macon's men? I know they're watching me. I slid down the tree, clutched my string of lights and walked slowly through the Thicket. I tried to keep calm, to think of pleasant things. I remembered seeing once a television commercial for a local utility company. A bowl of light bulbs arranged like pieces of fruit. Pineapple shoots made out of green neon tubes.

A twig snapped behind me. Something like a whisper. I ran through the dark.

———

6/15/88. Claire, here's my blind belief: you'll soon join the heroes and martyrs in the stars. The search for you will become the sole purpose of my observations. Any fuzzy object in the sky, any strange new phenomenon, I'll know what it is. Just remember: my southeastern aspect is blocked by lights from the mobile home park.

Tonight, Coma Berenices (according to myth, the hair of an ancient queen) blazes vigorously in my 'scope. The American astronomer Garrett Serviss, describing the constellation in one of his books, says it has a

> curious twinkling, as if gossamers spangled with dewdrops were entangled there. One might think the old woman of the nursery rhyme who went to sweep the cobwebs out of the sky had skipped this corner, or else that its delicate beauty had preserved it even from her housewifely instinct.

Well. Talk of domesticity makes you nervous, C, I know. But I remember your scattered hair, how you cut it the day you left to impress on me the seriousness and severity of your new life. How you left me to sweep it up. Now I wish I'd saved it, some little piece of you to touch.

6/29/88. I met a woman who looked like you. Last week Dalene took me to a party (my first trip into the city with her; we kept to the shadows so I wouldn't be overwhelmed all at once by the wild profusion of lights) and this woman, a foreign exchange student at Rice University, dancing with her husband, astonished me. I couldn't eat or drink. I sat in a chair overcome with desire, and watched her eyes, her lips, her hands. Later that night, making love with Dalene, I saw this woman's face, which was of course *your* face, in my mind . . . and pushed deeper and deeper toward you as far as I could go . . .

I carry an image of you in my head. I say I "see" you in my dreams. But creating and gazing at images is not the same thing as seeing. Image merely records/replaces what is absent.

7/20/88. "We were almost caught today. Azziz and I had stopped in a little town for tea. The hills all around us were being shelled – moderates versus extremists, though who can tell them apart? – but the city seemed safe. We sat in an outdoor café. I was reading the menu when someone shouted and pointed in our direction. A man in a market across the road. He'd recognized our faces – we hadn't realized that the local authorities had printed up posters. We ducked through the restaurant and escaped out the back. I was terrified.

"So I went ahead and bought the kerosene, Will. I'm going to perform my act sooner than I'd planned, while I still have the chance.

"Do you really not know why I'm doing it? Or are you trying to force me to face it? I can hear you now: 'Tell me, Claire . . . tell me what you want.'

"All right. I'll try. Yesterday in camp I was washing clothes with Selena, a beautiful sixteen-year-old who joined our outfit in Turkey. She has trouble pronouncing my name; I helped her practice. When she finally got it right, the word sounded urgent on her lips. *Claire.* I took her hand and put it on my breast. She squeezed me. I thought I'd faint. My knees shook, Will, no kidding.

"Me, the old woman of the group, utterly helpless in the hands of this child.

"She knew it, too, and whispered in English, 'You're mine now, Claire.' She grasped me hard by the arm and pulled me into her tent. Led me like a slave. And I loved every minute of it.

"It's not just with men, Will. That's what I'm trying to say – what you *want* me to say. With men I had an excuse – I was taught to bow to them. By my father, my crack-boned culture – encouraged to court their violence. But now I'm sure it's deeper, something in me – a desire to be erased. I've always felt it. You know I have. It frightens me. It gives me a thrill."

Skywatch, with the radio on. Coffee worse than usual.

Antares, the brightest star in Scorpio. A binary. Hard-to-find partner.

Heat waves rise off the ground, distorting what I see – soil and rocks, still warm from the sun, won't cool until ten. Lignite and natural gas swarm deep into the Thicket. The oil refinery's all the violence I want.

8/1/88. "This will be my last letter to you, Will. My task has been enormously complicated. For the past several weeks Azziz has been sulking because I've paid more attention to the women than to him. Then this morning I discovered I was pregnant. I've been queasy at dawn, feeling weak. This local doctor told me . . . never mind. The point is, Azziz – the only possible father – is ecstatic. He's asked me to forget my plan and to marry him."

(Our child, C, the little angel – last night I thought I saw him near the twin stars, Castor and Pollux. A faint object, I couldn't be sure . . . he dimmed, then disappeared . . .)

"I've decided to stick with my convictions."

I try to imagine what you'll look like – to extrapolate what I can't yet grasp from things I *have* experienced. Flames. Your body.

A mathematical model of fire. It must take into account the following variables:

1) The heat combustion of the volatiles.

2) The thermal conductivity of the char as a function of its mass retention fraction and temperature.

3) The specific heat of the char.

Where do you fit in this equation?

All that remains of the human body after cremation, I've read, is the canine maxilla, fragments of the parietals, occipitals, facial and palatal bones, ribs, vertebral drums and spine, the calceneum, the talus, and perhaps the tibial and humeral shafts.

To see a faint object, look away. It's there in the corner of your eye.

9/3/88. You feel dead to me, Claire. Are you dead? Solid in memory, no longer fluid as you were when your letters still came. The certainty of your presence, even at a distance from me, meant that the circumstances of our being together – past as well as future – could be changed, just as you could alter your appearance or opinions any time you liked.

Your death, on the other hand, illuminates – no, *contextualizes* – the past. Wrongly, perhaps. The cold, opposing currents that ran in you always can now be seen as a kind of order. A conflux of passions impelling you to sacrifice yourself as you did.

You stand in the middle of a square. Noisy brown children, chickens, dogs. One or two American cars. Slowly, you remove your dress, pulling it up over your head, revealing first your knees then your belly and breasts. You shake your short black hair. White skin, lightly tanned in the sun. Azziz hands you the kerosene. Lifting the can, you douse your face and shoulders. Rivulets run down your back, pool at your toes. Sad smile. Look of resolve. Then you open the matchbook, tear out a stick . . .

Two A.M., pyramid dark, I throw the switch. For a moment nothing happens – I fear a short in the circuit – then red lights, blurry in the mist, ignite the leaves of the trees. The woods sizzle, then flash. Houston dims, the chemical swamps simmer and boil. Barbed-wire melts, smoke begins to billow from the trailer home park. Families pour out, sweating. Macon's men run, steaming, from the bushes where they've hidden. The car lot bubbles and pops. Rust softens and flakes from tankers anchored in the shallows, mosquitoes spark into flame in midair. I'm peeling off my shirt. The bay's drying up. Come back to me, Claire, come back, my garden is charred, the beets have withered, the potatoes have burst. I close my eyes, my eyes, C, my goddamn open eyes −

———

The stars won't settle down until ten tonight. It takes that long for the ground to cool. Patience, more patience is what I've learned.

ACKNOWLEDGMENTS

My deepest thanks to Kathryn Lang, Keith Gregory, and Freddie Jane Goff at SMU Press for their diligence, patience, and dedication to literature; to Peter Copek and the OSU Center for the Humanities for a fellowship which gave me time to work on many of these pieces; and to the following people for their support and advice: Glenn Blake, Michelle Boisseau, Brandon Brown, Molly Brown, Rosellen Brown, Elizabeth Campbell, Jennifer C Cornell, Richard and Kristina Daniels, Gene and JoAnne Daugherty, Corrine Hales, Ehud Havazelet, Edward Hirsch, Garrett Hongo, T. R. Hummer, Ted Leeson, Philip Levine, George Manner, Antonya Nelson, Grace Paley, Marjorie Sandor, Maya Sonenberg, Charles and Debra Vetter, Gordon Weaver, and most especially to Martha Grace Low.

Martha Grace Low

A native of Midland, Texas, TRACY DAUGHERTY
received his B.A. and M.A. at Southern Methodist
University and his Ph.D. at the University of Houston,
where he studied with Donald Barthelme. His first
novel, *Desire Provoked*, won the Southwestern Book-
sellers' Texas Literary Award. His second novel, *What
Falls Away*, was the 1994 winner of the Associated
Writing Programs Award for the novel. His stories
have appeared in the *New Yorker*, *Gettysburg Review*,
Ontario Review, *Southwest Review*, *CutBank*, *Folio*,
and other literary magazines. In 1992 he received the
A. B. Guthrie Jr. Short Fiction Award. A former Bread
Loaf fellow and a Fulbright participant, he is an asso-
ciate professor of English at Oregon State University.